"I believe that women and men still have some basic differences,"

Clint said. "A true man will always be the hunter rather than the hunted, and I think most women like it that way."

"Really?" Debra countered. "And what characteristics make up the true woman, may I ask?"

He gave her a hooded look. "Oh, no you don't. I'm not going to start generalizing about women. If I keep one step ahead of you, I'll consider myself damn lucky."

She assumed an expression of playful sternness and hoped it masked how churned up she felt. "I intend to keep one step ahead of *you*, Clint Rasmussen. Maybe several!"

"Hmm, I wonder who'll win?" he asked softly.

Dear Reader,

Welcome to Silhouette—experience the magic of the wonderful world where two people fall in love. Meet heroines that will make you cheer for their happiness, and heroes (be they the boy next door or a handsome, mysterious stranger) who will win your heart. Silhouette Romance reflects the magic of love—sweeping you away with books that will make you laugh and cry, heartwarming, poignant stories that will move you time and time again.

In the coming months we're publishing romances by many of your all-time favorites, such as Diana Palmer, Brittany Young, Sondra Stanford and Annette Broadrick. Your response to these authors and our other Silhouette Romance authors has served as a touchstone for us, and we're pleased to bring you more books with Silhouette's distinctive medley of charm, wit and—above all—*romance*.

I hope you enjoy this book and the many stories to come. Experience the magic!

Sincerely,

Tara Hughes
Senior Editor
Silhouette Books

JOAN MARY HART

Stranger at the Wedding

Silhouette *Romance*

Published by Silhouette Books New York

America's Publisher of Contemporary Romance

SILHOUETTE BOOKS
300 E. 42nd St., New York, N.Y. 10017

ISBN: 0-373-08631-8

First Silhouette Books printing February 1989

Printed in the U.S.A.

Books by Joan Mary Hart

Silhouette Special Edition

More than a Mistress #440

Silhouette Romance

Stranger at the Wedding #631

JOAN MARY HART

For years Joan Mary Hart worked as an executive secretary, but her desire to be a writer was always in the back of her mind. Aided by a supportive writers' group and a wonderful teacher, she began to pursue her true interest and put pen to paper. Joan says she learned a great deal from writing her first novel, but she plans to keep that early effort safely tucked away in a cupboard. She was overjoyed when her continued hard work and devotion led to the publication of her next novel.

Like most writers, Joan's always been something of a bookworm and still remembers crying her way through *Black Beauty*. A longtime romance fan, she claims her own life measures up to the genre's fictional standards: she knew her husband of thirty-three years for a whirlwind *two weeks* before they married—and that was just the beginning of the adventure! For the next three years the romantic couple lived in Africa, then sojourned in Europe, South America, the Caribbean, the Orient, New Zealand and Australia. For now, the Canadian-born author and her husband reside in California.

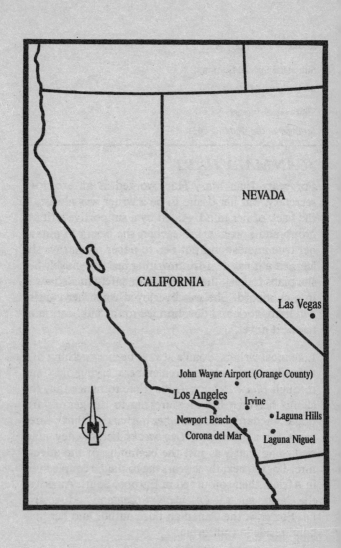

Chapter One

Silver centerpieces of white and lavender orchids on beds of fragrant orange blossoms blurred before Debra's eyes as the toast to the bride echoed around the banquet hall. Despite the June sun filtering through the sheer curtains of the Southern Californian beachfront hotel, she shivered. Resolute in her goal to conceal her misery, she took the required sip of champagne, though she had to stifle a cough against its bitterness. No one must guess her true feelings regarding Brian Hayward's marriage to Laurie Rasmussen, or she would have suffered this ordeal for nothing. Still, her lips trembled.

"It's terrible...just terrible the way Brian threw her over for the boss's daughter... Oh!"

The whisper and hasty shush pierced the lull following the toast at the table where Debra sat some distance from the bride and groom. Stunned, Debra knew she must have paled and, instinctively, she ignored the covert glances being sent her way. She tilted her chin, letting her pride mask the humiliation. Loose waves of auburn hair slid lower on her shoulders as she pretended the whisper was of little concern to her. An imperceptible sigh of thankfulness escaped her lips when a flurry of conversation rippled along the table. Everyone, it seemed, was intent on covering up the awkward silence.

Was that what everyone was saying? That she had been jilted? The shock of that thought dried any residue of moisture from her eyes.

Conscious of the man beside her shifting and glancing at her, she looked neither right nor left, and definitely not at Kathy, the clerk from her office who had made the faux pas. The poor girl was no doubt red-faced. But Debra knew Kathy could only be referring to her; and it hurt—oh, how it hurt.

Always hold your head high, Debra. Remember, you're the daughter of a marine. The voice of her beloved father rang through her head as she remembered his last advice to her before his fatal return to Vietnam. Even after all these years, the principles he had instilled in her gave her strength. Pride had brought her to Brian and Laurie's wedding; pride would see her through.

She took a steadying breath and set her glass on the table, then watched, horrified, as some champagne spilled over her shaking fingers onto the pristine damask. Through a haze of embarrassment, she was aware of the man beside her leaning toward her.

"Are you all right?" a deep, unfamiliar voice asked quietly.

While dabbing at the damp tablecloth with her napkin, she half turned toward the man. His solicitude was commendable, she supposed, but right now she would have preferred her clumsiness to have gone unnoticed.

"I'm fine, thank you," she said. Her green eyes lifted no higher than his broad, gray-suited shoulders before she dropped her napkin on the table and turned away from him.

"You don't look it. Fine, I mean."

For a second, Debra couldn't believe she had heard correctly, but the man's words were unmistakable. Temper flared through her at his cool, deliberate remark. She lifted her head and her gaze clashed with his. "I beg your pardon," she said, trying not to snap.

He made no immediate attempt to answer her. Instead, he lounged in his chair and returned her scrutiny, a faint, cynical smile on his thin lips. He was big, blond and handsome, although nowhere near as handsome as Brian, of course. Anyway, she'd never liked fair-haired Nordic men, especially the rugged outdoorsy type who made her own five feet five inches seem insignificant. He was taller than Brian, much taller. That was obvious. His shoulder brushing against hers was several inches above her own. A tiny scar ran through one sun-bleached eyebrow, giving him a perpetually quizzical look.

But it was his eyes that unnerved her and fanned her temper. Clear and blue, they stared back at her, his expression one of faint irritation—and pity.

She opened her mouth to squelch him once and for all, but he forestalled her.

"I must have been mistaken." He lifted a champagne bottle and held it over her glass. "More champagne?"

It was as if he realized his comment had been out of line and had decided to soften his approach. Her temper waning, Debra shook her head but thanked him. She must have imagined the pitying look. Good grief, she was getting paranoid, imagining that everyone knew. Unlike the others at the table, he was not from her office. She'd never seen him before. He was not the sort of man a woman would forget.

He shrugged his broad shoulders and sipped his champagne. With relief, Debra looked away, just as the music started and Brian and Laurie began circling the floor in the traditional first dance. Debra's hands tightened in her lap. Had she, in the past, looked as besotted as Laurie when she'd looked up at Brian? She hoped not, for that look was far too revealing. Any undercurrent of animosity she might have felt toward Brian's bride faded. The girl's love was there for all to see. As for Brian, he wore that lopsided smile that she still found so appealing.

To her dismay, Debra again felt tears burning the back of her eyes. She wondered how long she could keep up the pretense. How long could she hide that she felt brokenhearted and betrayed?

How could Brian say he loved her, then be so deceitful? What a fool she'd been, believing his lies! Suddenly the humiliation and hurt overwhelmed her resolve to conceal her distress; she couldn't withhold a small moan. When a large hand touched her bare arm, she jumped.

"Let's dance, shall we?"

It was that man again. Apparently he never gave up. She shook her head and pushed back her chair.

"No, I, ah, I'm leaving." She'd had enough. All she wanted to do was go home; the strain of hiding her feelings was more than she could stand. Besides, the perfume from the orange blossoms was giving her a headache.

She felt her chair removed from her back, and a strong, masculine hand curved around her elbow.

"Just one dance, hmm?" He towered above her as he bent to lift her seating card from the table. "How about it, Debra McLeod?"

Again she shook her head, then moved through the crowd milling and chatting on the fringes of the dance floor. Intent on reaching the door, she was flabbergasted when, seconds later, she felt his hand on her back and found herself, somehow, on the dance floor.

She looked up at him with undisguised resentment. "Are you always this pushy?"

Instantly he stopped dancing. His hands fell to his sides. Flustered, she stared up at him, her mouth open.

"If you feel that strongly, Red, far be it for me to push myself on you," he said with coldness.

"Oh, all right," she snapped, hurriedly stepping forward. She reached for his stiff, broad shoulder, not caring if she was making an about-face. She couldn't have another man drop her, not here, not right in the middle of the dance floor! "And don't call me Red."

The grim line around his mouth quivered, and he chuckled above her, his feet picking up the rhythm. As his hand slid down her back to her waist, a tingle of awareness shot through her and caught her by surprise.

His other hand drew hers close to his chest. "Surely you've been called Red before," he teased. His breath ruffled her hair in a gentle caress.

"Only when I was a child. I didn't like it then, and I don't like it now."

Again he chuckled, and she could feel the rumble of it in his chest as he pressed her closer to him. "I see you have the temper that goes with your hair, Debra McLeod." He pulled back and dipped his head low to look into her face. "Don't look so indignant. It could have been worse. I might have called you 'freckles.'"

"Debra is quite sufficient. Or better still, Miss McLeod."

His grin widened and deepened the laughter lines at the corners of his mouth. "You may call me Clint, Miss McLeod. Not that you've shown any curiosity as to my name. I find that quite shattering to my ego."

Her lips curved into a reluctant smile as she caught the full impact of his blue eyes. "I'd say you have a healthy ego. One setback won't hurt it."

"Ouch! Shame on you, Miss McLeod!" He pushed up her chin while still holding on to her hand, then nodded with some inner satisfaction. "Keep those sparks in your eyes. I was afraid you were going to burst into tears back there—" he inclined his head toward the banquet tables "—and I can't bear to see a woman cry. Makes me feel positively helpless."

"You were mistaken," she said icily.

He grinned. "If you say so."

Darn it, he was enjoying embarrassing her. To let him know he'd succeeded only put her at a further disadvantage. She forced a smile.

"You, helpless?" Her tone emulated the teasing note in his. "I don't believe it."

"Oh, but I can be, R—" He caught her warning glance. "Debra," he amended with a slight bow. "Wait until you get to know me better. Meanwhile, practice that smile. You're much too pretty to look downhearted."

"I am not downhearted. What's more, I will not be getting to know you better."

His arm tightened around her back. "Don't be too sure."

Blue eyes assessed her, making her squirm as they lingered a moment on her mouth and then drifted lower to the cleft between her high, small breasts that could be glimpsed beneath the ruffled V neckline of her dress. From his vantage point, he was seeing a darn sight more of her than she would have liked. The fact he seemed to admire what he saw only flustered her further. His supreme confidence increased her irritation, though she grudgingly recognized this was partly because Brian's defection had shaken her self-confidence.

She'd get this dance over with, then leave. She'd not have to see Clint after today. Her emotions were too bruised, too chaotic just now for her to cope with a persistent male.

Gradually she became aware of how comforting it was to feel his arm around her, to feel the warmth of his capable hand through her thin silk dress. She needed to be held just now, although she hated admitting that to herself. Even Clint's calling her pretty and giving her that all-male once-over made her feel better. Which only went to prove how contrary she could be—one second she condemned the man for his boldness, and the next minute she basked in it!

She'd taken great care with her appearance for this early-afternoon wedding. Blusher and bright coral lipstick had helped relieve her pallor. As for her dress, well, there she had really splurged. An exquisite emerald green, the dress looked deceptively plain on the hanger; but once she slipped it on, it gave her the air of sophistication she sought. It molded the contours of her figure without being blatant, and she loved the feel of the rich silk, a luxury she couldn't really afford. Today she needed the reassurance of knowing she looked well dressed. She needed every prop she could get to live through the agony of Brian marrying another woman.

The ache within her made her move closer to the man who held her. She couldn't help peering around Clint's broad shoulder to see Brian's dark head across the room.

"Admiring the bridal couple, Debra, or ogling the groom?" Clint asked in a cold, disapproving voice.

She gasped. "How dare you suggest—"

"You don't deny it, I notice," Clint observed dryly. "It's not done, you know. Ex-girlfriends shouldn't ogle the groom."

Debra stopped dancing, prepared to march off the floor. "Brian is a co-worker, nothing more."

"Really?" Clint kept dancing, and she was forced to follow. His grip on her clearly indicated he'd carry her around if she didn't dance willingly.

"You're wrong, you know," she said.

"Come off it, Red. Who do you think you're fooling? Not me, that's for damn sure. I was sitting beside you at the table, remember? I heard what that kid said."

"That doesn't prove anything."

"It proves you're upset, no matter how you try to hide it. Hell, why can't women accept it when an affair is over?"

"You're talking from experience, no doubt!"

He laughed softly and drew her resisting body closer to his. "You're a little fool," he muttered in her ear. "Why did you come today, feeling as you do?"

"To prove I don't care," she answered without thinking.

"You aren't doing a very good job of that, are you?"

She glared up at him. "So, I'm a lousy actress."

He gave her a speculative look. "Just how thick were you two?"

"That's none of your business," she flashed, still smarting from his crack that she wasn't convincing anyone she no longer cared for Brian. It didn't help that she suspected he might be right.

Clint sighed, looking bored, and this annoyed her further. Darned if she'd let him believe she'd acted like a lovesick fool over a man without good cause to feel that way.

"We were going to be married," she told him. "No one knew, except my mother."

"You mean Brian actually proposed?"

"Yes!" She felt insulted by Clint's obvious disbelief. "We'd been dating for over a year. I didn't know Brian was seeing Laurie. For the past few months he'd broken several dates with me, but I believed him when he said he was taking work home at night."

Although her revelation put Brian in a dreadful light, Debra was taken aback by the fury that darkened Clint's face.

"Which means," he said through his teeth, "that Brian was deceiving Laurie as well as you."

"I guess so," she retorted, "but she's the one marrying him." Debra was puzzled by his concern for Laurie. "I didn't know that Brian even knew Laurie until I received the wedding invitation."

"Where did he meet her?"

"Six months ago, Laurie's father bought the company where Brian and I work. I saw her there once when her father was showing her around." Debra lifted her shoulders. "Somehow, Brian must have wangled an introduction."

She looked up at Clint and caught a hint of compassion on his face. She immediately felt affronted. She wanted no man's compassion. Though she longed to give way to the hurt that was tearing at her insides, she would do that only in the privacy of her own home. After all, a marine's daughter didn't fall apart in public.

The music stopped just then, and Clint turned her around. His hand moved up her back and slid beneath the soft waves of her hair. When his fingers brushed her nape, she pulled away, but Clint exerted a subtle pressure on her shoulder and turned her toward Laurie and Brian.

"All right, look at him. Take a good look. Get him out of your system right now. He's married and no longer a part of your life."

"I know that!" Furious, she tried to free herself from his grasp, but he merely tightened his hold. Thwarted, she exclaimed, "What business is it of yours, anyway?"

"Maybe I object to the woman in my arms rubbernecking to look at another man."

The music started again, and Clint began to sway in time with the dreamy ballad. Agitated, Debra fell into step, determined to meet any challenge of his.

"Dented your ego again, did I?" she said through tight lips.

"Hmm, that pleases you, does it?" he murmured, the anger gone from his face, a knowing glint in his blue eyes as he looked down at her. He caressed the sensitive skin beneath her chin and laughed under his breath when she angrily pushed his hand away. "Nothing like a new man to make you forget the old one, Debra."

"Hah! That line must have come over on the *Mayflower*!"

He threw back his head and laughed. "Touché! I like a woman with spunk."

"I have plenty of spunk. And if you needle me much more, you'll find out just how spunky I can be!"

"Hey, you're scaring me, Red. Can you feel me quaking?"

He was trying to make her laugh. She knew that by the twinkle in his eyes. But she couldn't. As if in instinctive response to her mood, he sobered. "You could always pretend, Debra, just for this afternoon. It might do you good."

She held his gaze. "I don't use people, Clint."

"No, I don't imagine you do," he said thoughtfully, "but since I would be aware of what you're doing, you wouldn't really be using me, now would you?"

"Perhaps not." She avoided his intent look and fingered his lapel. She wished she could take this easy way out, but knew she wouldn't. She made herself look up. "I'm not getting involved, pretend or otherwise, with another man for a long, long time."

"You're too young to think that way," he scoffed, obviously amused. "Some man will change your mind. It may as well be me."

She frowned. "I'm twenty-six," she informed him, piqued by his levity when she had never felt more serious. "I don't make a habit of falling in love. Brian was the only man I ever thought of marrying."

"Well he won't be the last, will he?" Clint came back curtly, his mouth set. "Forget him. Don't let one bad experience sour you on men."

"I'm not! Just because I'm not interested in doing as you suggest is no reason to think that."

"That's what it looks like to me. Anyway, despite your avowals of love, I'm convinced it's your pride, not your heart, that's suffering."

"And of course, you're an authority on hurt pride and broken hearts."

He didn't counterattack. Instead he pulled her closer, making her aware of his powerful physique, his hard chest brushing against her softer curves. To her disgust, she felt her heartbeat quicken.

He gave her a sidelong glance. "Ignoring my offer to fill in, I see." His voice was softly teasing.

"I'm not looking for the next contender," she replied.

He laughed, but there was a certain smugness to his smile that made her wonder if he suspected she was not immune to him. What was the matter with her? It was Brian whom she loved. So why didn't she stop Clint's lighthearted flirting, once and for all?

She was vulnerable just now, that was why. Clint was making her feel like a desirable woman again—or at least a woman worthy of a man's notice.

She glanced up at him. This close, and beneath the light from the chandeliers, she could see a few gray hairs blending with the fair ones at his temples. He must be in his early thirties at least, she mused.

She was annoyed with herself for being curious about him. Without being too obvious, she tried to ease away from him.

"Now is not the time to exert your independence, Debra," Clint murmured. "Laurie and Brian are headed straight this way."

Debra felt her body tense and barely heard Clint's, "Hey, take it easy." Then, to her utter amazement, he bent down and pressed his lips ever so lightly to hers. His mouth on hers was soothing, and for a second, blotted out what faced her. When she realized what she was permitting, she jerked away.

"Of all the—"

But before Debra could berate him as she would have liked, Laurie's little-girl voice broke in.

"Now I know why you didn't sit with us at the head table, Clint," Laurie teased behind them.

Despite her anger with Clint for kissing her, Debra was grateful for his hand on her back as they both turned to face the bridal couple. Her lips still tingled from Clint's kiss, and her heart thumped wildly. But no wonder she was rattled. Half the people from her office must have witnessed that kiss. Clint wasn't the one who would have to withstand their curiosity come Monday morning.

The gist of Laurie's words suddenly penetrated. Why had Laurie expected Clint to sit at the head table? Surely such an honor was reserved for family members.

Clint stepped away from her to kiss Laurie on the cheek. "You're a beautiful bride, Laurie. Be happy, little one."

"I am." Laurie's blue eyes shone with affection.

Debra managed a polite smile, all the while wondering at the affection between these two. As for Brian, she couldn't look at him, or she'd break down. She'd extended obligatory congratulations in the reception line. She couldn't elaborate on them without feeling hypocritical.

She felt uncomfortable and guilty for her thoughts when Laurie's bright smile was turned on her.

"Debra, isn't it?" Laurie asked. "From Brian's office?"

"Yes," Debra replied, her lips stiff with the effort to smile. Laurie's hesitation over her name confirmed what she had suspected: Laurie knew nothing about her and Brian. She had suspected this when she received the wedding invitation. No bride would knowingly invite her groom's most recent girlfriend to their wedding.

Now Laurie wagged a playful finger at her. "Watch out for this brother of mine, Debra. He's a rogue with the ladies."

It was a miracle Debra didn't faint. "Brother?" she repeated as she stared accusingly at Clint.

A muscle worked in his cheek. "That's right, Debra. Clint Rasmussen."

Speechless, Debra was transfixed. Her mind whirled. Why had he hidden his relationship with Laurie? No wonder he had shown such concern for her.

Willpower, and willpower alone, made Debra turn from Clint to Laurie, and again Debra received a shock. She hadn't realized Laurie was so young; she couldn't be more than eighteen. Debra heaved a sigh. If her own distress hadn't monopolized her thoughts, she might have noticed Clint's resemblance to Laurie before. Both were tall and blond, their Swedish ancestry quite apparent.

"Didn't you know Clint was Laurie's brother?" Brian asked, his voice, with its false jocular note, a rude intrusion into her thoughts.

When Debra turned to face Brian, his brown eyes were sulky. He hadn't liked her ignoring him, hadn't liked it at all. Now, when she looked into his dark, handsome features, she was surprised her insides didn't turn over quite as she had expected they would.

Suddenly Debra was weary—weary of deceit and subterfuge. "No, I didn't know," she answered finally.

Then, with a murmured farewell to them all, Debra escaped through an open doorway to the lobby and headed, her pace increasing, for the wide glass doors leading outside. The thick maroon carpet muffled her footsteps and those of the man who caught up with her. He placed a now-familiar hand on her arm.

"Not so fast, Debra." Clint's voice was low and steady, but there were danger signals in his blue eyes when she looked up at him.

She sent him her most withering glance. "You deceived me. Purposely."

A flush tinged his cheeks. "Perhaps, but I'd have told you my full name if you had asked."

She laughed shortly. "That absolves you of nothing. You know full well I wouldn't have...confided in you if I had known." Her voice trailed away, and no matter how hard she tried to suppress it, some of the wretchedness she was feeling was evident.

He slipped an arm around her waist. "Look, Debra..."

She jerked away. "Keep your hands to yourself!"

"Lower your voice," he snapped in an undertone, "unless you want a row right here in the middle of the lobby." His nod indicated the people who watched them with avid curiosity from deep leather chairs.

She controlled the urge to tell him what she thought of him. As executive secretary to Mr. Johnson, the personnel manager of Rasmussen Products, she couldn't afford to be involved in a public scene with the owner's son.

As for Clint, he obviously didn't work for his father; Clint's name wasn't on the company's confidential organization chart. So where did he fit in? She hadn't even known the owner had a son.

Looking him up and down, she put all the disdain she could muster into her glance. "No, I don't want a row, or any other conversation, either."

She pivoted on her heel, determined to put distance between them, but Clint matched her stride. The minute they reached the spacious grounds and started down the pathway with its concealing border of six-foot red and white oleander bushes, she came to an abrupt halt and rounded on him.

"Leave me alone. There's nothing more to be said."

He shoved his hands into his pockets. "Come to dinner with me tomorrow. Give me a chance to make amends."

"Not a chance!"

She swung away from him, her heels clicking on the pavement. She tried to ignore him. After the blare of dance music, silence now seemed to envelop them, except for the faint rolling sound of the Pacific and the rustle of the oleander hedge, the sea breeze disturbing its abundant blossoms and poison-filled lush green foliage.

The minute Debra reached the parking lot, she waved her voucher in the air to attract the notice of the attendant who hurried over to take it from her. Throughout the whole byplay, she refused to look at Clint but was very aware of him beside her.

"Was my withholding my surname that big a deal?" Clint asked the second they were alone again.

"You know it was."

He sighed, dipping his head to one side so she was forced to meet his gaze. "If I had told you, you wouldn't have let me get to know you. You'd have run in the opposite direction."

"I don't run away from anyone, but I am choosy about my companions."

The words were out before she could stop them. She knew full well it was foolhardy to be rude to the owner's son, but anger overcame her normal caution.

She stepped forward as her blue Mustang emerged from the parked cars. Immediately the attendant vacated the driver's seat, and she tipped him generously while she froze with one glance Clint's instinctive movement to do so. Sliding behind the wheel, she locked the door, revved the engine, then lowered the window halfway.

"Goodbye, Mr. Rasmussen," she said coldly, closing the window before he could reply.

As she sped away, she watched him through the rear-view mirror. She was gratified to see him still standing there scowling, his hands jammed in his pockets.

Chapter Two

What was Clint's motive in choosing to sit beside her, instead of at the head table? The question nagged at Debra as she coped with the heavy traffic on Pacific Coast Highway, and the more she thought, the angrier she became. He definitely had some motive. He must have rearranged the seating to make certain he would be beside her when she arrived. At first she'd been too disturbed and heartsick to notice anyone, had been hardly aware of the big man next to her getting politely to his feet as she sat down.

Just then a Volkswagen, a surfboard strapped on its roof, cut in front of her. "Idiot!" she muttered and swerved into the inside lane.

The traffic thinned down once she turned inland on Crown Valley Parkway. Still, the near collision made her set her worries aside until she had reached her quiet cul-de-sac in Laguna Hills, with its neat town houses and their small, tidy front lawns.

She'd been a fool to confide in a complete stranger, to lay bare all her heartache. There had been something about Clint that had made her open up to him. So much for her judgment of men!

When she pulled into the garage, she was surprised to see her mother's yellow Toyota. Her mother usually worked all day Saturday at a souvenir shop in San Juan Capistrano, which was at its busiest on the weekends when tourists flocked to the mission.

"Mom," Debra called as she shut the front door behind her and hurried over the tiled entryway into the living room.

"Hello, dear, I've been waiting for you." Marilyn McLeod rose quickly from the sofa. Her attractive face seemed anxious within its frame of short auburn hair made lighter by a sprinkling of white. "I left work early. I knew you'd need someone to talk with when you got home."

Debra threw her arms around her mother's slim shoulders and hugged her tight. "You're always here when I need you. I'm very lucky." Her voice was husky with emotion.

"That's what mothers are for, dear." Marilyn returned the hug, then stepped back to search her daughter's face. "How about a cup of tea? It will make you feel better."

"Oh Mom, you always think a cup of tea will put everything right." Debra sent her mother a bleak smile.

"Blame it on an English mother and a Scottish father, Debra," her mother returned with forced cheerfulness.

Debra followed her mother into their small sunny kitchen. She was touched when she saw the rose, gold-rimmed tea service. A matching plate filled with chocolate chip cookies was set out on a tray and covered with an embroidered white cloth. The dainty china and cloth had been her grandmother's and were her mother's prized possessions. Her mother only used them on special occasions, or when she felt either of them needed a boost in morale. Today it was for her benefit, Debra knew.

Marilyn switched on the gas beneath the kettle, then turned to Debra. "You stayed at the wedding longer than I expected. I thought you'd put in an appearance, then leave."

"That's what I meant to do." Debra perched on one of the stools at the built-in breakfast bar. "But then the whole day turned into a fiasco."

"Oh? What happened?"

Debra launched into a recital of the day's events until the kettle whistled, and Marilyn turned away to make the tea. Debra waited until they were seated in the living room and her mother had filled their cups, before she continued. Her high heels kicked off, she relaxed for the first time that day. At the wedding she'd been too upset to eat anything, and now, comforted by a sympathetic listener and familiar surroundings, she sipped her tea and nibbled on one of the cookies she'd baked the other night.

Before long, though, she knew she'd have to respond to the spark of interest that appeared in her mother's eyes the second she mentioned Clint. She described him in the sketchiest of terms and then watched, with some resignation, the pleased look spread over her mother's face.

"Well, I don't think the day was quite the fiasco you implied," Marilyn remarked. "I like the sound of your Clint."

"Mother, he is *not* my Clint. Don't get any ideas. I am not interested."

Marilyn laughed. "Such vehemence!"

"I'd never go out with him."

"Never is a long time." Marilyn brushed cookie crumbs from her gray slacks and dropped them into the ceramic ashtray on the cocktail table. "Clint certainly sounds a lot more exciting to me than Brian. That man's wishy-washy."

"That's not fair, Mom," Debra chided. "You've taken a dislike to Brian, that's all, out of loyalty to me."

"I don't know how you can defend him," her mother grumbled. "Clint's right. Brian cheated on both of you girls."

Debra sighed and set her cup on the table. "I know. I hope Laurie never finds out. She'd be crushed. She's young and more vulnerable than I am."

"Is she?" Marilyn shook her head. "You're sensitive too, my dear, but you hide it behind an armor of pride, just as your father did. You know I didn't want you to subject yourself to this wedding today."

Debra threw up her hands. "I was doing fine until that remark of Kathy's. The idea the whole office is gossiping about Brian and me makes me cringe."

"Give them a week and they'll be gossiping about somebody else."

"I wish I could believe that, but I just can't," Debra exclaimed, still vividly aware of the humiliation she'd suffered. "Everyone is used to seeing me with Brian. We were a . . . a couple."

"You weren't wearing his ring," her mother pointed out not unkindly. "Nothing was definite, even if he did make a lot of promises."

Debra wrinkled her nose. "Promises, it seems, he never intended to keep."

Marilyn refilled their cups. "Am I being an interfering mother?" she asked hesitantly as she set the pretty china teapot on the tray. "Too outspoken, perhaps?"

"Of course not. I know it's because you care."

"I'm glad. I'd never want anything to come between us." Small worry lines creased Marilyn's forehead.

"Nothing ever will," Debra replied in a low voice. "You're my best friend."

Marilyn gave Debra an affectionate pat on the knee. "No mother could have a greater compliment."

Without the help of a husband, her mother hadn't had it easy, Debra thought. She and her mother had only had each other. Perhaps that explained the special rapport they shared as adults—a rapport nurtured over the years by mutual love and respect.

"Now, about the gossip at the office," Marilyn's voice broke into Debra's thoughts, "don't let it trouble you. From what you've told me, everyone is on your side."

"I don't want anyone taking sides or pitying me," Debra had to protest. "For a month I've had to put up with a kindness I don't want, people saying I'm better off without Brian. They've done everything but pat me on the head!"

"I'm glad to hear I'm not the only one," Marilyn told her with a wry grin.

"You're different. We're family."

"True, but..." Marilyn's voice trailed off. Something else was clearly on her mind. "Satisfy my curiosity about Clint, will you?" she prompted, looking far too innocent. "I know you say you dislike him—"

"Dislike him? The man is impossible! When I think what a fool he made of me, I could scream." Debra's toes curled into the deep rust carpeting. "I don't know anything about him, and that's the truth." She caught her mother eyeing her with amusement. "Okay, I admit most women would think Clint's a gorgeous hunk of a man, I won't deny that, but he tricked me. He knew about my involvement with Brian. I'm sure of it. Clint was...was lying in wait for me today. But why? That's what bothers me."

"Maybe you're imagining things." Marilyn drained her teacup. "Maybe he noticed you at church, then arranged to sit beside you at the reception. Maybe he just wanted to get to know you."

"No." Debra sat up straight and tried to ignore the sense of foreboding that was tightening the muscles in her neck. "It's not that simple. I'm sure of that."

"Well, you'll probably see him at the office." Marilyn looked delighted at the prospect.

Debra sighed. "Maybe."

When Marilyn lifted their empty cups onto the tray, Debra felt relieved that the questions about Clint were ended. Usually, confiding in her mother helped her with whatever problem she faced; but regardless of her mother's opinion, she couldn't forget Brian that easily.

Besides, after the underhanded way Clint had gained her confidence—and it had been underhanded no matter what he said—the single emotion she should feel toward Clint Rasmussen was hostility. And she did feel hostile. The less she saw of him, the better she'd like it.

Her mother was about to rise when the impulse to reveal her innermost yearnings to the one person who loved her made Debra place a detaining hand on her mother's shoulder.

"All I've ever wanted in a relationship was what you and Dad had together. I remember how happy you were when he came in from the base at night. I've always looked forward to someday having a marriage like yours." Debra propped her elbow on her knee, her chin in her hand. "I've worked hard to get where I am, but that's not enough, not for me." She smiled wistfully. "I want it all—a solid marriage and a successful career. Is that too much to expect?"

Her mother turned in her seat to face her. "I don't think so, Debra. The trick is in knowing which is the most important. I'm glad your father and I gave you an example of just how good marriage can be between people who love each other. He and I had so little time together, and you were so young when he . . . when he died."

"I didn't mean to revive sad memories for you, Mom." Distressed, Debra chewed at her lower lip.

"You didn't, dear. Your father is always with me," Marilyn replied quietly as she touched her heart.

"I know he is," Debra said softly.

A small silence ensued, and despite her mother's reassurances, Debra feared she had reawakened the tragedy in her mother's mind. Anxiety surged through her and didn't dissipate until a faint smile lifted her mother's brooding expression.

"It's perfectly natural, Debra, for a young woman to want a man to love, to want children. It's a basic, fundamental instinct. Where would the world be without it?"

Debra's lips curved upward. "How come I didn't inherit your common sense? You put everything in perspective. I'll bet I've been a pest lately, moping around the house."

"Well, you have been a bit gloomy," Marilyn agreed, then gave Debra a mischievous glance from the corner of her eye. "Don't brush this Clint Rasmussen off before I meet him, will you?"

"Don't plan on it." Debra shook her head vigorously. "You should have seen his face when I walked out on him today. Apparently he's not used to being refused. I doubt if he'll give me the chance to snub him again. Anyway, I have no intention of getting involved," she stressed, with the futile hope she could end any ideas her mother had on that score.

This time it was Debra who lifted the tray and padded, still in her stocking feet, into the kitchen.

Minutes later, as she hung her silk dress in the closet of her upstairs bedroom—an ultrafeminine room with white lace curtains and cornflower wallpaper—Debra wondered if Clint would phone her, despite her snub. His ego would be in for another jolt if he did. She would take great pleasure in delivering him another rebuff.

She rubbed the creases between her brows. Clint somehow managed to bring out the worst in her. She was never spiteful, yet here she was scheming to refuse a man's invitation before it had even been issued.

She went over to her ruffled vanity and peered into the mirror. Long tapered fingers ran lightly over a nose too short ever to be considered classical. Freckles, indeed! He should have seen her when she was in her teens. How she used to long to wash away her freckles, devouring every advertisement that promised to erase them. She'd never been brave enough to experiment, always afraid her mother's dire predictions would come true, that such creams might erase her skin as well. Now only a dusting of freckles remained over the bridge of her nose. She was so used to them she never noticed them.

Clint, it seemed, didn't miss anything. No matter how hard she had tried to disguise her unhappiness today, he had guessed she was miserable. His perceptiveness could prove dangerous for her should he become an opponent.

With an effort, she set aside her worries and put on a jogging suit before joining her mother in the living room to watch the six o'clock news. There was nothing uplifting, just the same old repetition of murders, demonstrations and wars.

Soon her mind turned to her own problems. When Brian returned to the office, it was going to be even more embarrassing for her than it had been after his engagement was announced. Well, she'd survived his wedding; she would survive this next hurdle, too. It was unfortunate he was Mr. Johnson's assistant. Under the circumstances, she would have to work with him. Once the office gossip died down, she hoped they could work together as amicably as they had in the past.

Debra recalled her elation when she'd been hired as executive secretary four years ago. She'd competed against numerous applicants. Her responsibilities and salary had increased rapidly as promised ever since. The only other woman with the same classification was Mrs. Langley, and she'd been with the former owners for twenty years. She now worked for Mr. John Rasmussen, Clint's father.

As executive secretary, Debra felt she had reached the first significant goal of her career. This was the best job she'd ever had, although she in no way felt confined to a secretarial position. As the company grew, so could the opportunities. She would stay.

And despite her penchant for tears earlier that day, she fell asleep later that night with only a single tear for Brian and the future they might have shared.

The next morning Debra slept late and had to rush to join her mother for church. Afterward, Marilyn left for San Juan Capistrano, the shop where she worked being open every Sunday from one until six.

Much as she loved her mother, Debra welcomed the solitude. She tied her hair back with a powder-blue ribbon, donned a pair of faded blue shorts and T-shirt, then wandered outdoors where she collected garden shears and a weeding fork from the garage. The trauma of the past month pushed aside for once, she felt quite content as she snipped away at the withered leaves of the red geraniums that bordered the front of their living room bay window. The minuscule front yard took little care. Most of the grounds surrounding the town houses were maintained by a home owner's association.

A mockingbird trilled away from atop a nearby eucalyptus tree as Debra knelt on a foam rubber pad to weed the crabgrass from their patch of lawn. When the inquisitive gray bird skimmed over her head to alight on a spiky pyracantha hedge, she sat back on her heels and watched it until, with a display of white-striped wings, it flew back to the eucalyptus to continue its serenade.

Her head was bent once more, her gloved hands busily tugging at weeds, when a resonant male voice destroyed her peace of mind.

"Why, Debra McLeod, you're full of surprises," Clint drawled behind her.

She jumped. Damn him! Why had he come when she looked an utter mess? She threw down her weeding fork and frowned at him.

She hadn't been wrong when she'd told her mother he was a gorgeous hunk of a man. From the cream Italian leather of his shoes planted next to her muddy gardening paraphernalia to the brown slacks that hugged his lean hips, from the tan knit shirt that accentuated his muscular chest and displayed the cords of his strong-looking arms, to the smile that was enough to make any woman go weak at the knees—he lived up to her description and more.

"What are you doing here?" she asked abruptly.

She started to scramble up when, without saying a word, he leaned over, circled her waist with those big hands of his, and set her on her feet. Immediately she pushed him away. She didn't want him touching her. She'd been taken in by one handsome man; there was no way she was going to repeat that mistake, although there was no similarity between the two men. Clint had a toughness, a maleness about him, that Brian would never possess. It made Clint all the more formidable.

With his neat, if casual, appearance drawing attention to her own earth-spattered shorts and top, she was in no mood to be polite. Yanking off her gardening gloves, she brushed a few grass blades from her knees. She waited for his answer, which he seemed in no hurry to give. Finally she had to look up. His eyes were laughing at her.

He shrugged. "I decided you'd hang up if I phoned, so I came by instead."

His glance swept over her, making her conscious of the tightness of her top across her breasts, the scantiness of her shorts, the expanse of bare legs on view.

She was annoyed by his look. "If you knew I'd hang up, didn't that tell you anything?"

Any trace of humor disappeared from his face. She glimpsed a flash of temper in his clear blue eyes an instant before they became expressionless.

"I wanted to come, and I did."

"Well, come in, then." She was being ungracious, she knew, but he had played her for a fool at the wedding. Just thinking about it made her boil. She started toward the front door but had taken only a few steps when she turned around to retrieve her gardening tools and saw Clint pick them up from the ground. "You'll get dirty," she exclaimed, reaching out to take them from him.

He held them away from her. "Where do you keep them, in the garage?"

"Yes, but—"

"An ex-farm boy like me isn't afraid of a little mud. Quit fussing, Red. I'll put them away."

He turned and walked around the corner to the garage. Debra hesitated a second, then went indoors, leaving the front door open behind her. She must at least wash her hands and face.

One look in the bathroom mirror confirmed her fears. She looked nothing like the sophisticated woman of yesterday. With her lip gloss eaten off at lunch and her face flushed from the sun, she looked years younger than she was. It wasn't the image she wanted to portray around Clint, but she refused to slap on makeup and possibly give him the idea she was doing it for his benefit. His conceit didn't need inflating.

Clint looked very much at ease when she walked into the kitchen. For some reason that irritated her further. He seemed bent on invading her life whether she wanted it or not. He washed his hands at the sink, then dried them on a towel while she stood in the doorway watching him.

"Making yourself at home, I see," she said curtly.

He grinned. "Why do I get this feeling you're not pleased to see me?"

She refrained from answering. He was in her house. She should at least be courteous.

"I, ah, thank you for putting the tools away." She took a couple of steps forward, then became aware of how crowded the kitchen seemed when a six-foot-two man took up more than his share of the space. She licked her lips. "Would you like coffee, a cool drink?"

"A cool drink will be fine," he told her with a faint smile as he folded the towel over the rack in the cupboard under the sink.

She hesitated. He was blocking the way to the refrigerator. When she gestured that she wanted to get past him, he stepped aside.

"Will you be more comfortable if I wait in the living room?" he asked, all politeness now.

She bristled at the hint of mockery behind his question. "Perhaps that would be best."

Without another word he sauntered past her, giving her a whiff of after-shave.

When she entered the living room carrying a tray with two glasses of lemonade, he came and took it from her. He set it down on the cocktail table and handed her a glass, then took one himself. He didn't sit down, but gestured toward the framed snapshot on the stereo.

"Is this you and your parents when you were a child?" he asked. When she nodded, he again studied the photograph. "Is your father a career marine?"

"He was." She didn't elaborate, but when Clint's gaze held hers she was forced to explain. "He was killed in Vietnam." Eyes pensive, she stared at the photograph. How distinguished her father used to look in his uniform, even though before the picture was taken he'd plopped his hat on her head. She remembered how he had laughed at her own youthful self-importance at wearing her daddy's hat, especially when it had slid down to balance on her ears. "I adored him," she said into a silence that now seemed too long.

With his free hand, Clint tipped up her chin. "I imagine he adored his little girl, too." His smile was indulgent, his eyes penetrating. "You must have been young at the time."

"I was five." She moved away from him and gestured for him to sit down. When Clint looked at her like that, she felt she could relax her guard. It was a feeling that she must control. She'd made that mistake yesterday; she wouldn't make it again. Too much about this man remained a mystery.

He waited until she was sitting in one of the wing chairs before he made himself comfortable on the sofa, his long legs stretched out before him and crossed at the ankles. He took a deep swallow of his lemonade.

"I was there for eighteen months near the end of the war," he told her, his eyes shadowed, as if he looked back on those years with reluctance and some pain. "Have you any brothers and sisters?" he asked in an abrupt change of subject.

She shook her head and wondered what he was thinking as he fell silent. A sudden frown furrowed his brow as he glanced around, then he waved his hand to encompass the homey room—cherry-wood tables glowing with polish, Wedgwood-blue floral sofa and solid-blue wing chairs plumply cushioned. "I had no idea being an executive secretary was this lucrative."

She took immediate exception to the suspicion in his tone and glance. "My mother and I share the expenses of this town house." She set her glass on the table between them. "Satisfied?"

His teeth flashed white in his tanned face, and he laughed suddenly. "You live with your mother? That must have cramped Brian's style."

It had caused numerous arguments with Brian, but she wasn't about to admit that to Clint. "Living alone, neither Mom nor I could afford this town house. I see no reason to desert my mother simply because it's the 'thing to do' for a woman my age to live alone or share an apartment with a friend. Mom and I happen to enjoy each other's company."

"Hey," Clint protested, leaning forward to set his empty glass beside hers, "don't misunderstand me. I think it's great." Again he sat back, a hard look now around his mouth. "I'm certain, though, that Brian didn't share my view. The more I learn about my new brother-in-law, the less I like. He'd better treat Laurie right, or he'll have me to deal with.''

Debra threw up her head in exasperation. ''I'm getting awfully tired of hearing about, and talking about Brian; but there is one thing I'd like to know. You knew about Brian and me before yesterday, didn't you?'' Her eyes challenged him to deny it.

''Yes.'' His answer was clipped.

''Did Brian give you my address?'' Her tone showed her displeasure at that possibility.

''Hardly! I got it from the personnel file.''

Her frown deepened. ''I've never seen you at the office, and no one else has either, or I'd have heard.''

The narrowing of his eyes was the only barometer that indicated he resented the implication of her remark. ''For your information, Debra, I went into the office on a Saturday and used Dad's master key to open the personnel files.''

''Oh!'' How she longed to blast him for prying into her records, but darned if she'd give him the satisfaction of knowing how much it infuriated her. Still, the effort required to curb her temper wouldn't permit her to remain placidly seated. She got to her feet. ''You schemed to sit beside me. You pretended you had to read my seating card to learn my name.''

''I was looking out for my sister's interests.''

He rose and destroyed the advantage of height that she'd enjoyed. Still, he seemed uncomfortable. A vein beat in his temple, and his shoulders moved impatiently. She felt certain he wished he could shrug off their whole discussion. Clint apparently didn't care for half-truths any more than she did, though he had deemed it expedient the previous day.

"What did you think I'd do?" she flared at him. "Did you think I'd throw myself at Brian for Pete's sake?"

A thin line of white teeth showed as he gritted out his reply. "Something like that."

She shook her head, unable to make sense out of what he was saying. "You can't be serious!"

He raked his fingers through his close-cropped blond hair but made no reply.

Her nails bit into her palms. "What, or should I say, who gave you that impression?"

"Look, Debra, there's no point in this interrogation." He gripped her upper arms firmly, although his thumbs caressed her soft flesh. "I was misled. You're far too proud to have caused a scene at the wedding."

She tore from his grasp. "Thanks for nothing! That you could even think such a thing is an insult!"

He spread his hands. "I apologize, okay? Cool down! I didn't come here to fight."

"Didn't you? You have a strange way of avoiding a fight. What's more, quit dodging my question. It was Brian, wasn't it, who gave you the impression I'd cause trouble." She swallowed, outraged. "He knows it isn't true," she burst out.

Sighing, Clint folded his arms across his chest. He looked big, strong and indestructible.

"You won't let it rest, will you?" he asked quietly. "If knowing hurts you like hell, you still want to know."

"Yes." All her hurt, all her angry frustration were there in that one word.

He settled his hands on her shoulders, then, and massaged them gently. "Sit down and I'll tell you all about it." He almost crooned the words. "Don't stand here all tense, ready to battle me. I'm not your enemy, Debra."

His whole attitude was geared to mollify her anger, and although tempted, she wasn't about to accept any olive branch. As if she, of all people, would make a spectacle of herself at the wedding! It was unthinkable! She was more than ready to do battle if need be, but she complied with his urging and sat on the sofa. When he settled close beside her, she was dismayed. His arm, stretched along the sofa back, disconcerted her.

"I'll start from the beginning," he told her, and lifted a strand of her hair that had escaped her ribbon. Gently he tucked it behind her ear. "I came home a week ago and discovered little was known about Brian, except that he worked for my father. Dad tried to talk Laurie out of getting married because she's so young, but she said she'd elope to Las Vegas with Brian if they had to. Against his better judgment, Dad gave his blessing. He had nothing against Brian, but I wanted to know more about the man who was marrying my sister."

"Surely your father wanted to know more," she murmured, shifting on the sofa until there was a more respectable distance between them. "The marriage was sudden."

Clint frowned at her. "He did, but this new company takes most of his time. He read Brian's file, but that was hardly sufficient. I promised I'd check on Brian at the places he and Laurie frequented. I knew nothing about you then and avoided going into the office during business hours. Above all, I didn't want to cast suspicion on my sister's prospective husband and cause talk."

"How considerate of you," Debra observed tartly. That she might be hurt by unnecessary talk clearly didn't matter. "Laurie doesn't know a thing about your investigation, I'll bet."

"That's right." The dangerous glint in his eyes warned her that he took exception to her tone. "The whole idea was to protect Laurie from hurt, not add to it."

"Where do I fit in all this detective work?"

"Someone let your name slip," Clint told her bluntly. "When it happened a second time, I confronted Brian. He said—" Clint shot her a quick glance, then lifted her hand and squeezed it.

"Go on," Debra ordered, tone abrupt. "Don't stop now."

"He said you wouldn't accept the breakup, that you pestered him to continue your relationship." Clint scowled, and it was plain he hated making the disclosure. "I realize now that he was covering up his own duplicity."

"How could he!" Rage whipped through Debra, and for a brief second she covered her face with her hands.

Clint must have misunderstood her emotion, for he drew her to him and cradled her head against his chest, his free hand smoothing over her hair. "Quit being brave. If you want to cry, go ahead."

"I don't want to," she denied furiously, a few tears dampening the front of his knit shirt. "I'm just so damn mad!"

"Of course you are." He stroked her back.

She knew she should pull away from him, but instead her arms slid around his waist, bringing her closer to him. With her cheek pressed against his chest, she could hear the steady beat of his heart, and somehow it calmed her. But only for a moment. She was all too aware of his hands on her back, as well as other sensations she couldn't or wouldn't define. She pushed lightly against his chest and sat up, letting her hands fall to her lap.

She avoided his eyes, then took a deep breath and made herself face him. "Sorry about that." She waved a hand that threatened to tremble. "I don't usually snuggle up to the first available male."

"Stop it, Debra! There's nothing wrong with needing the comfort of another human being."

"Perhaps." She wished he'd leave. She felt confused, and hated the feeling. She struggled for something to say, something to turn the attention on him and not on her own transparent face. "I didn't know Mr. Rasmussen had a son. I've never heard your name mentioned."

Her remark elicited a rueful smile from Clint. "I've been in Brazil for the past eight months, though I have a house here. Hotel living gets to be a drag." He shrugged. "You're right, I don't work for my father. I've formed my own engineering company. We specialize in troubleshooting."

"So if a company has an engineering problem, they call on you to solve it?" Thank goodness she was regaining control of her emotions. Even so, she sounded more composed than she felt.

He nodded. "Actually, while I'm here, Dad wants me to check into a problem he has. I'll be coming into the office."

Oh Lord, she would have to see him again.

"What are you going to do, Debra?" he asked. The expression in his eyes softened as his gaze flicked over her scrubbed face, then lingered on her mouth.

She moistened her lips and caught the sudden gleam in Clint's eyes. "Do?" she asked, wishing he wouldn't look at her that way, yet finding it provocative.

He got impatiently to his feet and moved away from her, then turned to stare down at her, his expression hard and unreadable. "Quit your job. Get right away before Brian returns from the honeymoon."

"Quit my job," she repeated, frowning. "Why should I?"

"Because it will be awkward for you if you don't, that's why." He gave her a sharp look. "Don't tell me you want to be here, waiting for him?"

"I'm not waiting for Brian!"

"Well, then . . ." Grim lines etched his mouth.

A slow-burning anger began to stir inside her, but she allowed no outward sign to alert Clint. She uncrossed her slim legs, and Clint's eyes followed the movement. Taking her time, she rose to her feet and settled her hands on her hips.

"Looking out for your sister's interests again, Clint?" Her voice was frigid. "I assure you, it isn't necessary. No matter what Brian has said, I don't run after men, and certainly not married ones."

"Don't be ridiculous! I don't think that. Can't you see you're prolonging your heartache by working in the same office with Brian? You should make a clean break."

"That's your opinion." She tilted her head proudly. "What I do is none of your business."

He knit his sun-bleached brows. "I'm making it mine."

Debra's hands slid from her hips and clenched at her side. "Don't threaten me!"

"Threaten you? Don't be silly. I'm trying to talk some sense into that stubborn head of yours, that's all."

Without deigning to answer that remark, which she considered as insulting as the ones that had preceded it, Debra stalked right past him, crossed the tiled entryway and reached for the front door handle. Before opening the door, she turned to find Clint close behind her.

"I am not quitting my job to suit you or Brian or anyone else! You can't scare me off, Clint Rasmussen, and if you try to, I'll fight you. That's a promise."

"Are you declaring war on me, Red?" His tone was ominous.

"If you want to think that, go ahead. And I told you before, don't call me Red!"

"Fond of issuing orders, aren't you?" He leaned past her; his hand closed over hers. The pressure of his hand didn't squeeze her fingers against the doorknob, or hurt her, but he opened the door. "I've done my best to protect Laurie, but it appears she's not the only woman who needs protecting where Brian's concerned."

"Bighearted, aren't you? I assure you I can take care of myself."

He stared down at her, his very height making her feel vulnerable. A soft smile appeared briefly on his face, then disappeared.

"Can you?" he murmured. "I wonder." Then all signs of softness faded and his mouth was once again unyielding. "Just remember, *Red*, if it's war with me you want, I warn you, I mean to win."

Chapter Three

War, was it? Debra banged her fist against the closed door. Clint Rasmussen would soon find she was no pushover. They'd soon see who was the winner!

She had no intention of leaving a perfectly good job just to please him. The man's nerve was unbelievable!

Her legs were shaking, an aftermath of her temper, and she returned to the living room to sink onto the sofa. Once again motive had ruled Clint's actions. Again his real interest and concern was Laurie. While she could understand, even respect his protectiveness toward his younger sister, Debra objected—and objected strenuously—to being cast in the role of the other woman!

It would be hilarious, if it wasn't so insulting. Clint might say he realized Brian's scheme was to shift all blame on her, but Clint's actions belied his words. He still must have reservations about her, or he wouldn't be trying to scare her off. By trying to make her quit her job, he was giving credence to Brian's lie.

The bile rose in her throat as she smarted from that slur. Clint obviously didn't credit her with any code of honor. What's more, the havoc his plans might have on her life certainly didn't trouble him, so long as he got rid of her. He had no compunction at applying a little soft soap if it coaxed her to do his bidding. It had all been pretense—his interest in her home life, his concern for her when he revealed the magnitude of Brian's double-dealing.

And she had almost been taken in by his seeming concern. She groaned with self-disgust. Gullible, that's what she was.

Just then, something compelled her to hurry to the window. A sleek, silver Lincoln Continental was turning the corner at the top of her street. Just the sort of car he would drive. Expensive. Elegant. His women were probably in the same category. They wouldn't be caught on their knees weeding in a garden. And she was darn sure he wouldn't put a brotherly arm around them!

She swung away from the window, grabbed their glasses from the cocktail table, then stomped through to the kitchen where she jammed them into the dishwasher. The machine wasn't quite full, but she dumped in some detergent and flipped the switch. The din of the dishwasher dispelled the silence, but nothing could dispel her feeling of emptiness.

"Blast him!"

She couldn't withhold the outburst. If Clint had lingered a second longer, she might have hit him and to the devil with the consequences.

And there would have been consequences. She didn't doubt that for a second. He was a ruthless so-and-so!

She tapped a finger against her compressed lips. Her intention of refusing any dinner invitation from him had never had a chance to be implemented. He hadn't repeated his invitation. That bothered her more than it should have. She couldn't help wondering whether, if given the chance, she would have accepted rather than rejected such an invitation. Her reason for accepting would, of course, be curiosity and nothing more.

That hardly mattered now. What did matter was that Clint should learn that she could be every bit as hard-headed and determined as he was.

A painful, choking laugh gurgled in her throat. Girls would be wearing bikinis in the Arctic before she'd quit!

Eager for the fray, she reported ten minutes early for work on Monday morning. She had expected the company to be renamed when the senior Mr. Rasmussen took control, and it had—Rasmussen Products. But that wasn't the only change. The company's business of supplying flexible ducting and other sundry parts to the aerospace field was flourishing. The long, low building had been repainted. New desks and file cabinets had been purchased for the engineering, sales and data processing departments, while carpenters were busy enlarging and modernizing the factory in the rear of the building.

Debra greeted the dark-eyed receptionist with a jaunty wave and smiled her "good morning" to everyone she passed on her way along the corridor to her office. Already two men were waiting for her in personnel, and she handed them employment applications to complete.

When Kathy delivered the mail an hour later, Debra made a point of chatting with her. Kathy stuttered at first and couldn't meet her eyes, but Debra pretended not to notice. By the time the teenager left, Debra felt satisfied that any self-consciousness between them over the incident at the wedding reception had been overcome, although neither of them brought up the subject.

It was at the midmorning coffee break in the cafeteria that Debra heard the first mention of Clint and the wedding. Surprisingly it didn't prove as embarrassing as she had expected. Her best friend at the office, Sharon, and two secretaries from other departments, were more interested in questioning Debra about Clint than dwelling on her former relationship with Brian. She was noncommittal, careful this time not to fuel any gossip.

Her determination to thwart Clint in any plan he might have to remove her from her position lost much of its impetus when he didn't put in an appearance. It was Thursday before the office grapevine forewarned her of his arrival.

At eleven-thirty on that day, Mr. Johnson called her into his office. "Mr. Clint Rasmussen wishes to give some dictation and has specifically asked for you, Debra." He gave her a keen look. "The senior Mr. Rasmussen has left unexpectedly for London. His son has agreed to fill in for the time being. Please assist him in any way you can."

She hid her dismay. "Certainly, Mr. Johnson."

It appeared Clint would be in the office more often than he or she had anticipated. Or wanted, in her case. Mr. Johnson was probably wondering why Clint didn't have Mrs. Langley, his father's secretary, take his dictation.

If she wasn't mistaken, Debra thought, round two in their battle of wills was about to begin.

She took the time to go into the ladies room to freshen her lipstick and run a brush through her thick, glossy hair. With critical eyes, she examined her tailored, brown-and-white-striped shirtdress, straightening the stand-up collar and narrow belt. Yes, she thought, she looked cool and businesslike, just the way she intended to be from now on in any encounters with Clint Rasmussen.

Ten minutes later, outwardly calm, she walked across the plush green carpeting of the president's reception office. Mrs. Langley looked up from the lone desk in the spacious room, a tiny frown of concern on her pleasant face.

"Debra, what took you so long?" she asked in a low, worried voice, turning her well-coiffed gray head to glance at the closed door behind her. "Mr. Rasmussen has checked with me twice to see what's keeping you."

"Sorry, Janet," Debra murmured, though her apology was for upsetting Mrs. Langley and not for keeping Clint waiting. He could wait all day as far as she was concerned; but she liked Mrs. Langley and was sorry if her tardiness had caused the older woman some anxiety. Business matters necessitated they speak over the phone to each other almost daily, though the president's office and the personnel office were at different ends of the building.

From Mrs. Langley's manner, Debra was positive that the other woman had no suspicion that the summons to Clint's office probably had nothing to do with business.

When Mrs. Langley announced her arrival over the intercom, Debra readied herself for the coming encounter. Her fingers tightened on her notebook when Clint's deep voice came over the line.

"Turned up, has she, Mrs. Langley? Send her in, please."

The polite smile with which Debra took her leave of the other secretary vanished when Debra stepped inside Clint's office. A feeling of claustrophobia engulfed her the instant she shut the door behind her. Still she managed a cool, impersonal glance for the man rising behind the desk. Sunlight shone through the wall of windows at his back, throwing his face into shadow and creating a halo effect around his fair head. Debra almost laughed aloud at that thought. Clint was definitely no angel!

He wore a blue-and-gray tweed sport jacket and gray slacks, with a deep maroon tie adding the right touch of color against his white shirt. She suspected he preferred this less formal attire than a business suit and would please himself rather than follow convention.

He looked quite accustomed to occupying such an impressive office, with its rich leather chairs, huge mahogany desk and floor-to-ceiling bookcases. She studied him unobtrusively and, for the first time, thought how dignified he was, distinguished even—a description she didn't bestow lightly.

Now his eyes roved over her from the top of her auburn hair to the tips of her high-heeled pumps. "Very efficient looking, but I wouldn't have thought it professional to keep your boss waiting."

The rebuke registered and, what's more, irritated her. He was right, though she didn't like the "boss" bit. Technically he wasn't even her employer, let alone her boss!

"Nothing to say, Debra?" he prompted, a slow smile spreading from his lips to his eyes. "Not even 'good morning'?"

"Good morning, Mr. Rasmussen." She crossed the room, conscious of his eyes on her the whole time.

He indicated one of the leather chairs in front of his desk. "Sit down, please."

She sat, crossed her feet neatly at the ankles and flipped open her notebook. Then, pencil poised, she returned his stare. His was amused, hers was as blank as she could make it.

He shook his head, then reached a long arm over to snatch the notebook from her and toss it on his desk. It was the first indication he was becoming annoyed.

He'd startled her, but except for a sharply indrawn breath, she stifled any objection to his high-handedness and merely arched her brows at him.

"I can't take dictation without a notebook," she pointed out as she smoothed her dress over her knees.

He folded his arms on his desk and leaned toward her. "That was an excuse to get you in here, and you know it. We have to talk."

"Talk away." She lifted one shoulder and tried to look bored.

"Keep it up, Debra, and I'll come over there and kiss you—and kiss you hard," he threatened, lips flattened against his teeth. "Then we'll see how cold and impersonal you can be."

"Here? In the office? You wouldn't dare." She flashed him a superior smile, despite the topsy-turvy state of her stomach.

"Oh, wouldn't I?" He got to his feet and started around the corner of his desk, his stride purposeful.

She jumped up and backed away. "I warn you, you touch me and I'll scream the place down!"

She wished she could retract her words the moment they were uttered. Heaven's, she sounded like an outraged virgin in a Victorian melodrama!

Obviously taken aback, Clint halted, then laughed. Much to her relief, he returned to his high-backed leather chair. His smile bordered on a smirk as he waved a hand and indicated she should follow suit. He waited until she sat down before he leaned his elbows on his desk. The magnetic pull of his steady gaze increased her feeling of disquiet, yet she couldn't look away.

"Why, I do believe I've managed to shake your cool, Miss McLeod."

"You don't shake my cool," she retorted. "You annoy me, that's all."

"I was right about the temper."

"Aren't you right about everything?" She couldn't keep the bitterness from her voice.

"Don't get carried away, Red." There was an edge to his tone. "In case you've forgotten, you work for me."

"I do not!" She glared at him. "I work for your father's company. You may be sitting behind your father's desk, but don't let it go to your head."

"Why you insulting little—" He took a deep breath. "If I say you're insubordinate, you'd be out the door, and fast."

Once again she jumped to her feet, and this time not from fear, but fury. How dare he use his position in their private war! "Then do it. I'm not sitting here parrying insults with you." She grabbed her notebook and spun on her heel.

"Come back here!"

She ignored him and heard him swear under his breath, heard his chair bang against his desk. She was not surprised when he strode past her and insinuated himself between her and the door.

"You're not walking out on me again, Debra."

She wanted to yell "watch me", but it was pointless. She couldn't walk through him. To take the confrontation to that stage would cause repercussions she didn't want to think about. She wanted no physical contact with this man.

She set her hands on her hips. "I obviously can't overpower you, but I don't have to listen to you, either."

"My God, you're stubborn."

One brow rose as she looked him up and down for a change. "Used to women capitulating, are you?"

"On occasion."

"This must be a new experience." She allowed herself a light laugh.

He didn't look amused. He was too busy struggling with his temper. "We'll go out to lunch and see if some food will improve your disposition." He caught her look. "All right, our dispositions. We have things to discuss rationally. Like finding you another job."

"I wondered when you'd get around to that." Disregarding her instincts to avoid their touching, she patted his cheek. "Forget it, big man, I'm not going anywhere."

"Brave, suddenly, aren't you?" Grudging humor lurked in his eyes and countered somewhat the grimness of his mouth.

"Not suddenly." She slanted him a look from beneath black lashes. "You're finally meeting the real me. I'm not given to emotions, despite what happened last Saturday. You shouldn't allow that single incident to give you a false impression of me."

"And what do you think my impression is?" he mocked.

"That I'm a defenseless female just waiting for a macho male like you to rescue me from myself. I'm not like that at all." She was beginning to feel rather foolish analyzing herself for his benefit, but she kept her face deadpan and hoped Clint didn't suspect how she felt.

Much to her chagrin, he laughed. "Defenseless? You?" He shook his head. "Sensitive, yes, and I find that rather endearing, much more so than that poker-faced secretary who marched in here awhile ago."

"That's only because a poker-faced secretary poses more problems for you."

"None that I can't handle," he drawled, "in case you've forgotten."

She needed no reminding of his threat to kiss her, and involuntarily her eyes went to his lips. Beneath her gaze they softened.

"Wishing you'd accepted the challenge?"

The audacity of that taunt jerked her gaze to his. The suggestive gleam in his eyes increased her inner upheaval. Somehow she managed a bland smile.

"By no means," she replied calmly and with the right degree of amusement.

"Putting your emotions in cold storage, are you? Or, perhaps you're hoping 'pretty boy' will come back to thaw you out?"

So she had been right. He did think that. She gritted her teeth. "You obnoxious—!"

"Why, Debra, I can almost read your mind. Such naughty, naughty words."

"There isn't one in my vocabulary that's low enough," she retorted in a furious whisper, the sudden murmur of voices outside reminding her of the secretary sitting no more than twenty feet from the other side of the closed door. "Now, will you get out of my way and let me leave."

"Not yet. We've come to no decisions about lunch or your job." He took the two peaks of her collar in his hands and tugged slightly. "How about it, lunch and a quiet, sensible discussion?"

She smiled sweetly into his face. "No."

His jaw hardened. "Why not?"

He sounded curious, as if her repeated refusals to go out with him and to quit her job were designed for no other reason than to annoy him. This man had a hard time taking "no" for an answer.

She brushed his hands away. "I'm not going into that again. I have a good job and I'm not quitting. That's final."

"Why be difficult? I'll see to it that you get another good job, a better one even. I've spent most of this week lining up a position for you most secretaries would grab in a minute."

"You really shouldn't have put yourself out." She glared at him and put her free hand onto her hip in a stance of flagrant defiance. "Offer the job to someone else. *I am not interested*. It would be a pity for all your hard work to go to waste."

"Damn it, Debra, I don't have all day to pander to your obstinacy." He grabbed her arms, the suddenness of which caused her to drop her notebook and pencils. His firm grasp made it obvious he didn't intend she should push him away as she had done earlier. Angry blue eyes returned her glare, then he swept a glance down the length of her, his gaze riveting on the agitated rise and fall of her breasts. In a split second the atmosphere changed. His mouth remained grimly determined, but there was a hint of desire in his eyes as he pulled her hard against him. "Hell, why am I arguing with you?" he asked hoarsely. "All I've wanted to do since you walked in here was this." His mouth came down on hers, hot and demanding.

She couldn't pretend that she was taken totally by surprise. That man/woman awareness had been between them the second she'd entered his office. No, even before that, much as she might want to deny it. Still, she struggled, pride and temper demanding it. Physical attraction wasn't going to rule her life, or allow him any power over her actions.

Her hands were trapped uselessly against his broad chest while she twisted and turned. She was conscious of his lips, softer now, moving over hers, of his hands releasing her arms to caress her back. The thin fabric of her dress rustled as he pulled her closer. Her soft, feminine body molded perfectly into his hard, angular frame.

Despite her resolutions to the contrary, she found herself sliding her hands up his chest, delighting in the feel of warm skin beneath fine cotton, the springy texture of his hair as her hands clasped behind his neck. She sighed her satisfaction as he deepened their kiss. With her body bent back over his arm, she had to cling to hold onto him. When he lifted his head they were both gasping for air, but pride made her boldly upbraid him.

"If you think a...a kiss will make me give in and quit, you're wrong."

She wanted to sound angry, disgusted. Instead her voice was husky and shaken, even to her own ears. She would have settled for at least sounding composed, pretending the kiss they had shared had had no effect on her, when in reality she had been disappointed when it ended. Shame flooded through her at that reluctant admission. She should have stopped him, but just how, she had no idea.

He kissed the tip of her nose. "Honey, you're far too serious." A sexy grin made fun of her attempt to resume their argument. "That kiss was inevitable, and we both know it." He rubbed his lips across hers in a way that was gently teasing and provocative. "Hmm, you taste good." His breath was warm on her lips.

"Clint, stop." She turned her face away. "If you really don't have any dictation, I have to get back to my office."

He wasn't clutching her to him, but when she tried to step free, he held her there easily.

Leaning over her, he nuzzled his cheek against her hair. "Such a practical girl. All business, even when you're in a clinch with the boss." Laughter laced his words.

"I don't want to be in a clinch with you," she retorted, bolstering her anger, needing it to combat the sweet lethargy attacking her limbs.

He chuckled and pushed her hair aside with his cheek so he could nibble her earlobe. "Next time I'll pick somewhere more private, I promise."

"Darn you, Clint Rasmussen, there won't be a next time." She broke free.

"Oh, yes there will." He watched her as she straightened her dress. "That was the appetizer." Once again he leaned over her, this time to whisper in her ear. "Didn't it whet your appetite, honey? It did mine."

"You—"

"Running out of names to call me? It must be tiresome having to act the lady when you'd like to clobber me over the head." He grinned at her.

"At least you know it! That's something!"

"I know more about you, I'm beginning to think, than you know yourself," he told her, his expression suddenly serious. He moved aside, leaving her path to the door unobstructed. With a sweep of his hand he gathered up her notebook and pencils from the floor and handed them to her.

"It seems pointless to insist on lunch in your present mood," he said. "I doubt you'd agree to quitting."

"I'm glad you've finally accepted I mean what I say."

Her retort was sharper than it might have been. The sweetness of success, of making him accept the reality that she had no intention of quitting on demand, wilted beneath the realization that he didn't care whether she had lunch with him or not, if no purpose of his was satisfied by the arrangement.

"Don't feel too pleased with yourself," Clint told her dryly as she brushed past him. "I always have a contingency plan."

Chapter Four

For the umpteenth time Debra's fingers hit the wrong typewriter keys, and for the umpteenth time she blamed Clint, even while knowing she was being unreasonable. His parting shot about a contingency plan was making her positively uneasy. No wonder she was typing like a high school girl at her first typing class.

He couldn't get her fired, no matter how hard he tried, she reasoned. At every performance review, she'd been commended for her efficiency. Oh, he could use his influence to discredit her, but somehow she didn't think he would stoop to that level. No, she suspected he intended making her uncomfortable, perhaps embarrassing her in some way at the office so that she'd want to quit. Well, if that was his plan, he didn't know her nature as well as he imagined he did. She could take any heat he intended dishing out! She would not cave in and let him run rough-shod over her.

"Are you going to the aerobics class tonight, Debra?"

With a start, Debra looked up from her typewriter. "Hi, Sharon. Yes, I'm going." She glanced at her wristwatch. "I had no idea it was five already."

"Well it is, so let's go or we'll be late," her tall, curly-headed friend scolded.

"Be right with you." Debra covered her typewriter and pushed back her chair. "Did you drive this morning, or do you need a lift?"

"I'd appreciate a lift," Sharon replied. "My car is still in the garage. Dave dropped me off this morning. He's even promised to have dinner ready when I get home."

"Now that's the kind of husband to have," Debra teased as they walked out to her car, surprised at her own pang of envy.

She and Sharon chatted in a desultory fashion during the short drive south on the San Diego Freeway. Leaving the freeway at Irvine Center Drive, they drove through what appeared to be open countryside, though multistoried office buildings could be seen in the distance. As always, Debra enjoyed this part of the drive to Laguna Hills, enjoyed the sight of orange groves, their neat rows in sharp contrast to the windbreak of eucalyptus trees. Peeling bark exposed the pinkish-gray trunks of these lofty sentinels, here and there their branches trailing untidily to the ground.

She glanced off to the left. No brown smog clung to the base of Saddleback Mountain as sometimes happened. The mountain looked exceptionally beautiful tonight, she thought, silhouetted against a cloudless cerulean sky.

It was Sharon's voice that dragged her attention from the view. "Does it still hurt when you think of Brian?" her friend asked hesitantly.

"No, I'm getting over Brian." Debra experienced a faint shock when she realized how Clint had usurped Brian from her mind. "Someone told me it was my pride, not my heart, that was affected." She wrinkled her nose. "He might have been right."

"He?"

Debra sent Sharon a sheepish grin. For all her intention of being closemouthed about Clint, she couldn't carry it off with Sharon now that they were alone and there were no inquisitive co-workers around to overhear. Sharon was a true friend. At the wedding Debra had been grateful that Sharon and Dave had come over to her the minute she'd arrived at the church and had sat beside her throughout the service. She'd missed their moral support when they'd been seated at different tables at the reception.

"It was Clint Rasmussen," she admitted.

"You mean he knows about you and Brian?" Sharon sounded aghast.

"Unfortunately, yes." Debra drove to a small shopping center a few streets from her home. She drew up opposite the corner storefront. "We have five minutes until class starts," she told Sharon.

Conversation about Clint or anything else was, of necessity, halted as she and Sharon grabbed their leotards and hurried indoors, both intent on finding an empty change cubicle.

"Be careful, Debra," Sharon said in a low voice as, some minutes later, they took their places in the lines of leotard-clad women already warming up with a variety of exercises. "I don't know Clint, but in the circumstances, he must disapprove of your working with his brother-in-law."

Debra clasped her waist and began bending side to side. "I know that, but he'll just have to accept it."

"Perhaps." Sharon gave a faint grunt as she touched her toes. "Just remember he's the owner's son."

"I'll try."

Sudden music drowned out Debra's attempt at flippancy. The shapely female instructor had put on a record, and chatting stopped as rows of women followed her lead into the intial head roll and stretching exercise.

It was ironic, Debra mused, that without knowing all the ins and outs, Sharon could see right away that Clint would object to her working with Brian. If the truth were known, there were others who thought the same thing.

Well, she could see their point, could understood why Clint wanted her to quit, but that did not change her resolve to thwart his intentions. She couldn't let Clint win in their battle of wills, not when he obviously harbored the thought she'd cause trouble in his sister's brand-new marriage. She felt degraded by that opinion. He deserved to have her dig in and fight.

A matter of pride, perhaps. So be it. She could see nothing wrong with being proud. Her father had been the proudest of men, and Clint certainly had his share of that commodity. Everything considered, she and Clint were bound to clash.

On the way home an hour later, Debra avoided further talk about Clint, and Sharon took the hint. Later that evening, Debra found it more difficult to avoid her mother's questions, especially when she told her Clint had come into the office that day. She held back from mentioning Clint's threats regarding her employment. To upset her mother without being certain of Clint's ultimate intentions was pointless. Besides, her mother was disposed to like Clint, sight unseen. Strangely enough, she had no wish to change that opinion, although it was becoming increasingly improbable that her mother would ever meet him.

Debra was still thinking about Clint when she went to bed shortly after eleven. There was no point fooling herself, his interest in her was predicated on her association with Brian. Immediately her mind rejected that unflattering thought. Clint definitely hadn't been thinking of Brian when he'd kissed her today.

Neither, for that matter, had she. It was demoralizing to admit how Clint's kisses might puncture her resolve in any confrontation. But it wasn't just the chemistry between them that had her worried. In the few instances when Clint and she had engaged in repartee, she had delighted in his sense of humor, his wit. She was dangerously attracted to him, and the attraction went far deeper than the mere physical.

If only they'd met some other time, without the insurmountable problems now besetting them, the outcome of their meeting might have been different.

She awoke the next morning determined to set aside her wishful thinking, and steeled herself for further conflict. Clint had insulted her and she mustn't forget it. He would put his contingency plan into effect soon. Brian and Laurie would return from their honeymoon in another week.

Friday came and went, as did the weekend and the early part of the next week. Not once did Clint put in an appearance. Every day she bolstered herself to defend her position, then came home feeling flat, like a fighter who had trained for a bout that never occurred.

When Mr. Johnson called her into his office the first thing on Thursday morning, she had a premonition it had something to do with Clint.

Mr. Johnson beamed at her through his thick glasses. "Debra, I have to congratulate you on the excellent work you did for Mr. Rasmussen last week. He was most appreciative."

"Why, thank you, Mr. Johnson." What had Clint told him for Pete's sake? She felt awful accepting congratulations she hadn't earned.

"Much as I hate to lose you, I've agreed to Mr. Clint Rasmussen's request that you be promoted to Mrs. Langley's position."

Shock held her silent a moment. "Is Mrs. Langley leaving?" she exclaimed finally.

Mr. Johnson nodded. "Mrs. Langley informed me a few days ago that she'd like to retire. Her husband retired last month, and he's keen for her to do the same."

Debra sat back in her chair. Her immediate fears were unfounded; Clint hadn't removed Mrs. Langley from her position simply to find a niche for Debra far removed from Brian. In her heart, she knew he would never do something so unprincipled.

"When the senior Mr. Rasmussen left last week, he informed me he could be gone a month," Mr. Johnson told her. "His son has assumed his position in the interim."

No way would she work with Clint Rasmussen for a month! She had to convince Mr. Johnson she didn't want the promotion; he was going to think she was out of her mind. Clever, clever Clint. Debra could feel the anger building inside her at the way he had maneuvered her into this impossible situation.

"I'd hate to leave personnel, Mr. Johnson." She leaned forward. "I like the contact with the public, and the college classes I've been taking these past years have all been geared toward personnel." She clasped her hands in her lap and hoped he would accept her reasons without argument.

As she expected, Mr. Johnson looked astounded. "You don't want the promotion?"

She shook her head. "No." Her tone was definite.

He pursed his lips. "You surprise me. I judged you to be an ambitious young woman."

"I am, but—"

Mr. Johnson removed his glasses and wiped them on a tissue. "Debra, why not give this promotion a trial run? If later on you are unhappy with it, for any reason, come and see me." He paused to put on his glasses again. "You'll receive a substantial increase in salary." He mentioned a sum that made Debra gasp.

Debra chewed at her lower lip. She supposed it could put Mr. Johnson in an awkward position if she refused the promotion. It could also jeopardize her career, if she stayed with this company, for her to turn down such an opportunity. Nobody would understand, or worse still, everyone might think she wanted to remain in personnel because of Brian. She'd been truthful when she said she liked public contact, but it wasn't a strong enough reason to turn down a promotion as executive secretary to the owner of the company and his son, especially considering the salary involved.

Mr. Johnson was aware that she'd been dating his assistant. For that reason alone he might be relieved this promotion was in the offing. Brian had married the owner's daughter, after all.

"Very well, Mr. Johnson, I accept. I suppose it would seem foolish to refuse."

"You'll be glad you did, I'm sure." Again he beamed at her; she could feel his relief.

"When does this change take place?" She forced herself to sound pleased.

"Monday. With the senior Mr. Rasmussen being away, you'll have a chance to ease into your duties. I'm sure you'll find the younger Mr. Rasmussen understanding."

She doubted that. Anyway, it wasn't the new position that worried her, but Mr. Johnson wasn't to know that. It was the thought of working closely with Clint for a month that was unnerving her and making her wonder what new surprises he had in store for her.

Smiling faintly at Mr. Johnson, she rose. She had liked working for the personnel manager, and it helped to realize that he sincerely believed the change of position was in her best interests. He didn't know Clint had instigated the promotion for ulterior reasons.

And could instigate other changes if he felt inclined. The man's gall had no limits.

Back at her desk she phoned Mrs. Langley to request, in her best secretarial manner, for an appointment to see Clint. In less than five minutes Mrs. Langley rang back and told her Clint could see her immediately.

Debra marched up to the president's office where she thanked Mrs. Langley politely for her congratulations, surprised at the speed with which Mr. Johnson had phoned the news of her acceptance. Her mind awhirl with the coming showdown with Clint, Debra nevertheless wished Mrs. Langley all the best on her retirement.

"My husband's happy about my decision," Mrs. Langley confided, "and I know I'm leaving the two Mr. Rasmussens in good hands."

Debra smiled her appreciation of Mrs. Langley's compliment, but minutes later when the door to Clint's office shut behind her, Debra's furious green eyes drilled him from across the room. He had been sitting at his desk in his shirt sleeves and reached for a jacket that lay over an empty chair as she bore down on him.

"How dare you!" she cried. "Of all the underhanded, low tricks!"

He shouldered his way into his deep brown suit jacket. "Not happy about your promotion, I gather," he drawled, not in the least perturbed by her attack.

"Oh, you're so smart, aren't you?" Her breath was coming in spurts, her temper out of control now that she was actually facing him. Filled with resentment, she felt disgusted that in spite of everything her heart was racing and her palms were clammy. The memory of being held in his arms in this very office flashed through her head and wouldn't be dislodged. He looked all-powerful, a virile male in the prime of life when no one and nothing could daunt him. It was that aura of supreme arrogance that drove her to be her most insulting. "Couldn't do your own dirty work, could you, Clint? You had to have Mr. Johnson do it for you."

"Only you would call a promotion my 'dirty work,' but I should have expected this harangue."

"I dislike being manipulated!"

"That's your fault. You left me no alternative."

"No alternative!" Her hands balled into fists. "What right have you to pass judgment and sentence on me? You're a conniving, interfering, b—"

"Debra," his voice thundered across hers. "Keep a civil tongue in your head when you speak to me, or you won't have a job to complain about."

"Threatening me again?" she threw back restlessly.

He strode toward her, white lines of temper about his mouth. Grabbing her upper arm, he swung her around and propelled her toward the door.

"Not threats, Debra. This time you've gone too far."

The sharp toe of her pump caught him squarely in the calf. He swore under his breath, stopping dead, making her stumble against him. He turned to scowl furiously into her mutinous face. Blue eyes blazed into hers, his grip on her arm was painful.

"Don't start something you can't finish, Debra."

She was panting with temper. "What have I to lose? You've just fired me. I'll say what I please."

"Will you? Will you indeed?" His square jaw tautened; his eyes leaped with temper. "What do you think I'll be doing while you're hurling insults at my head?"

Exhilaration, half fear, half daring, surged through her at the menace in his tone. She'd scratched beneath his urbane outer shell; she delighted in it and didn't care what happened next. He'd ruffled her often enough; now it was her turn.

She tossed back her head, auburn hair flying. "Just what can you do, big man, hit me?"

"Don't tempt me! There's a first time for everything!"

"Oh, but that isn't your style, is it Clint? You do everything with finesse. Like rearranging other people's careers to suit your own ends."

He released her arm and stepped back from her, his broad chest rising and falling as he heaved a sigh. "Sarcasm doesn't suit you, Debra."

Her resentment at the injustice of it all got the better of her, and her lips trembled. "Sarcasm! You object to my sarcasm?" She infused strength into her voice in the hope Clint hadn't noticed her momentary loss of composure. "How do you think I feel, being run out of a job I like just because I made the mistake of being involved with the owner's son-in-law *before* his marriage?" She gave a small wave of her hand. "Now this so-called promotion has been withdrawn because I had the effrontery to object to your methods."

Clint pulled at his collar. "It's not like that and you know it." His hand was gentle when he touched her shoulder. "Come on, Debra, sit down. Let's start over again, and this time let's not throw insults at each other."

Shaken by the force of her anger, she allowed him to guide her into a deep leather chair. Some of her hot anger was cooling down to a simmer. She still felt she'd been wronged but was willing to listen. Her hand shook when she smoothed her royal blue skirt over her knees as she crossed her legs.

Clint had resumed his seat behind his desk. She was conscious of his eyes, no longer hostile, drifting over the tailored white blouse she wore with its button-to-the-neck simplicity.

"Would it be that difficult for you, Debra," he asked quietly, "to work for me? I've never been accused of being an ogre."

There was a teasing note in his voice, obviously meant to disarm her. It wasn't going to work. Unsmiling, she faced him, her chin thrust out.

"You've used the advantages of your position unjustly, Clint." She couldn't be positive, but she thought she saw him wince.

Still, he answered without hesitation. "I gave you your chance to leave gracefully. You didn't take it."

"How magnanimous of you. Quit or else." She drummed her fingers on the arm of her chair. "A double standard, though, isn't it? I've worked for this company longer than Brian. Did you know that? Did you even care? I notice you've made no mention of Brian changing his job, or of a convenient promotion for him."

"Brian is a personnel assistant. There was nowhere else he could be assigned, short of the manager's position. Your case is different. You know damn well a good executive secretary can get a job anywhere. Don't imply I gave Brian preferential treatment because he's a man. Good

Lord, woman, I've given you the best secretarial position in the firm and an increase in salary. What more do you want?"

"To be left alone!" she cried passionately. "To earn my way honestly with no devious reasons behind any promotion." She pushed forward to the edge of her chair. "Can't you understand? I don't want my career subject to your whims!"

His lips clamped together. He looked ready to explode. "Whim, is it? Oh, it's much more than a whim. I want you where I can keep an eye on you. Is that blunt enough for you?"

"Keep an eye on me! Oh, you've got nerve!"

He laughed, a harsh, rasping sound. "Maybe I should rephrase that to keeping an eye on Brian."

"Why do you continually pair me with Brian?" she exclaimed. "How often must I tell you our . . . our involvement ended with his marriage?"

For a minute Clint just sat there watching her. "I'd like to believe that, Debra." He lifted a pencil and snapped it between his fingers. "Brian was seeing a couple of other women besides you and my sister these past few months. He's a woman chaser."

Her shock was total, and her eyes widened in disbelief. "I had no idea," she whispered. "Are you sure?"

He nodded. "I didn't learn this until after the wedding. As for Laurie, well, the damage is done. I can only hope Brian will reform, that he really loves Laurie. For the time I'm here I'll be watching Brian, and watching him closely."

Debra was affronted by the warning look Clint gave her, as if he were including her with Brian again. "A lot of good that will do Laurie once you take off," she retorted.

"I'm not taking off, not yet. I have several, ah, goals to reach before then." His eyes were coolly enigmatic.

"Anything could happen in a month, Debra," he told her, a sudden gleam in his blue eyes.

"I suppose so." She looked down at her hands folded in her lap. "Does Mr. Johnson know your real reasons for this promotion? Does your father know about Brian and me?"

"No. No to both questions."

She sighed with abject relief. She couldn't have borne it if they had known. Clint would have had his way, she would have had to quit. As it was, it appeared he had won this round. She started to rise.

"Debra, don't run off."

Clint's soft drawl stopped her, made her meet his gaze once again. "Yes?" she asked, determinedly impersonal.

He leaned his forearms on his desk. "Come out to dinner with me tonight?"

She gave him a straight look. "Why should I, after you've..." She shrugged. She'd voiced her objections to his actions already and wasn't repeating them.

"Don't say no," he coaxed softly. "Don't you think it's time we met on neutral ground? Why, you might find out I'm not such a bad fellow after all." He smiled beguilingly at her.

She felt her insides respond as she'd come to expect them to whenever he went out of his way to charm her. She knew she shouldn't accept, knew she should refuse in a way that would put an end to his ever asking her out again. She couldn't afford to get involved with another man from the office. One, moreover, who would stop at nothing to get his own way.

Words of rejection threatened to spill from her lips. Her anger toward him was perfectly justified. She could write a list of reasons why she should have nothing to do with this man, but her curiosity could not be denied.

A tiny, reluctant smile crossed her face. Curiosity, what an anemic word! She knew she wanted to spend time with him away from the office, wanted to meet him on neutral ground. Maybe if she went out with him she could break the strange power he was weaving over her.

"All right." She purposely showed no emotion either way and knew by the surprise in his eyes that he'd been prepared to persuade her. She was rather proud of her outward calm, yet annoyed with herself for looking forward to the evening in his company.

"I'll pick you up at your home around seven," he said, "that way you won't have to worry about your car."

"Fine."

As usual, Clint thought of everything. Still, she was glad they weren't leaving from the office. She wasn't dressed for an evening at some smart restaurant. A date with Clint would involve, she was certain, one of the more elegant establishments where one didn't go without a reservation.

Once again his blue eyes took in her tailored appearance. In that instant she shelved her earlier decision to always appear businesslike whenever in his presence. After all, a date with Clint Rasmussen definitely warranted her wearing the most sophisticated dress in her wardrobe!

Chapter Five

Debra, may I come in?'' her mother called.

Debra smiled to herself. She'd been expecting a knock on her bedroom door ever since she'd left a note on the downstairs entryway table telling her mother she had a date with Clint and wouldn't be home for dinner. This was one of the evenings her mother worked an extra hour at the shop, and Debra would normally have cooked dinner. Whenever Debra had a date on that night, her mother usually went right into the kitchen upon arriving home. Right now, though, Debra knew her mother's curiosity was the reason she was hotfooting it upstairs.

Debra opened the door. "Come in, Mom. Just don't remind me that I've changed my mind about Clint."

Her mother laughed. "Well, you know what they say— a woman has a right to change her mind."

Debra's smile was rueful. "I really meant it at the time when I said I'd never go out with him, but the man's persistent."

Again her mother laughed as she plopped down on the pale blue bedspread of Debra's narrow bed. "I like a man who knows what he wants and goes after it."

"I don't think Clint allows many obstacles to thwart him," Debra returned dryly. "Besides, I suppose I should get to know him better. I should find out what I'm up against."

"Goodness, Debra, what an attitude!"

"I'm just being realistic, Mom."

Debra opened the sliding door of her closet and flipped through her modest array of dresses and separates until she found the dress she wanted—a black lace creation that she'd planned to wear from the instant Clint had given her that assessing look in his office. She'd already had her shower, applied her makeup and donned black lingerie in preparation.

Slipping off her short kimono, she stepped into the dress. When Debra glanced in the mirror, she sighed with satisfaction and smoothed the dress over her hips. Delicate lace skimmed the tips of her shoulders and curved down into a wide scoop neck. The hemline border of two deep flounces added a frivolous touch to an otherwise straight skirt. The flounces brushed the top of her knees and emphasized the slenderness of her legs.

The dress was sophisticated—a dress a woman wore when she wanted to attract a man's attention. Debra bit her bottom lip, suddenly undecided. Perhaps she was courting trouble, perhaps Clint would consider her appearance in such an outfit as an open invitation, or worse, a come-on.

She glanced at her mother's face which registered approval, and Debra mentally chided herself for her moment's hesitation.

Somehow she had always managed to fend off Brian's more amorous advances. A reticence in her nature had always stopped her from taking that irrevocable step. But there was something about Clint that made her unsure of how she would react given the same circumstances. His kisses and touch aroused her in a way that was frightening.

As close as she was with her mother, Debra could not share her doubts; they were far too personal. Instead she told her mother about her promotion. Marilyn was thrilled for her and seemed unconcerned about Clint's reasons for his action. She went on to chat about the events in her day before going downstairs to make her dinner.

Not long afterward, Debra heard the door chimes and Clint's deep voice. Anticipation made her hands tremble as she slipped her small, pearl, drop earrings in place and reached for the matching pendant, a spray of pearls on a long, narrow, gold chain. Costume jewelry, certainly, but the set looked perfect with her dress.

She pressed a hand to her stomach. Why was she so nervous? She was no schoolgirl on a first date. Looking in the mirror, she checked her appearance for the last time, then dabbed perfume on her wrists, pleased her mother had given her the expensive scent the previous Christmas.

In case it should become chilly later in the evening, she draped a crocheted black sweater over her arm, then lifted her small, black patent clutch and started down the stairs. As she passed the landing, the open plan of the living room gave her a clear picture of Clint's neatly brushed blond head bent attentively toward her mother's. She wondered what they could be discussing to look so engrossed, then forgot the question when they both turned toward her.

Clint's gray suit had a faint blue pinstripe through it and looked terrific on him, especially with the pale blue silk shirt and midnight-blue tie he was wearing. She loved blue. That thought made her look into his eyes, and immediately she wished she hadn't. He was looking at her as if she were a particularly delectable dessert he couldn't wait to sample.

She was crazy to go out with him. What madness had made her accept? If it wasn't already too late, she would have found some excuse and stayed home. She held her breath as he left her mother's side and strode toward her and up two steps to take her hand. His long, low whistle came as a complete surprise and made her laugh, releasing her tension.

"You look lovely," he drawled. "That's a very pretty dress."

She smiled to hide her attack of nerves. "Why, thank you for the compliment, kind sir." Color flooded her cheeks as his gaze drifted down to her legs, in fashionable dark hose, and feet, in spike-heeled black patent sandals.

When his eyes lifted, she knew he couldn't miss the pink in her cheeks, and she was unsurprised to see his lips quirk. Before he could make any remark, her mother coughed discreetly, and Clint turned toward her.

"Have a nice evening, you two," Marilyn said, all but shooing them to the door. "I'll probably be out when you get home, Debra. I'm playing bridge at the Nelson's tonight."

Debra wondered why her mother hadn't mentioned before that her bridge night had changed, then forgot all about it as she and Clint made their farewells. She knew by the look on her mother's face that her mother had taken to Clint, which Debra felt happy about. It wasn't simply because this made everything more pleasant all around, either. Somehow it seemed important that her mother should like Clint, but she purposely didn't examine her reasons.

"Hey, come back here," a deep voice chided, making her turn her head against the soft, gray leather headrest of Clint's car to look at the man who, lately, was never out of her thoughts. "What are you thinking about?" he asked.

She smiled at him. "I was thinking how you and Mom seemed to be getting along so well when I came downstairs. You were absorbed in conversation."

He lifted one shoulder. "We were getting acquainted."

"I'm glad. Mom's always hospitable, but she usually reserves judgment of my men friends at first."

"Have there been legions of them, then?" There was more than a hint of sarcasm in his tone.

"Don't be silly," she scoffed, taking offense before she saw the straight line of his mouth relax.

He headed the silver Lincoln Continental toward the coast. "I've never had a woman call me silly before." He sounded amused.

"Too intimidated, probably," she answered back, grinning.

His teeth flashed. "But you're not?"

"Definitely not!"

He gave her a devilish glance out of the corner of his eye. "Good. That isn't what I want you to feel when you think about me."

It was her turn to give him a sidelong glance. "Always supposing that I think of you at all."

He tut-tutted at her. "I haven't fed you yet. You'd better be good."

"Oh, I will be." She paused deliberately. "I'm starved."

He laughed, merging the Lincoln into the Pacific Coast Highway traffic. "Aren't you curious to know what emotion I want you to feel?"

She looked straight ahead. "No."

He chuckled deep in his throat, making Debra's own lips twitch with amusement.

"You're a dreadful tease," she pretended to complain. "You're baiting me."

"Perhaps," he said, "then perhaps not."

She stroked the soft leather of the padded armrests between them. "This is a beautiful car."

"I like it." His glance mocked her for the change of subject.

In that moment Debra dismissed any misgivings she'd had at accepting Clint's invitation. She was glad she had come. If it wasn't for the attraction stirring deep within her whenever she was with him, she could even have relaxed. For once, antagonism was not spoiling their time together.

Was he as aware of her as she was of him? If she was reading his hints correctly, it seemed possible. Where this could lead them she didn't know, but for tonight she was determined not to worry about it or anything else. She was going to enjoy being with the most exciting man she had ever met.

The nearer they got to Newport Beach, the more congested the traffic became. Debra let Clint wrestle with the traffic without disturbing him with chitchat.

When he turned into the busy parking lot of one of the restaurants situated on the harbor, she was sure they'd wait an hour for a table, even with a reservation. But with an unobtrusive passage of some bills, Clint got a table by a window. Shore lights illuminated the boats that glided past.

Despite the people crowding into the cocktail lounge and dining room, he had somehow secured for them a private enclave cordoned off by hanging greenery and well-placed screens. Except for the piano music and the murmur of voices, they might have been alone.

"I don't know how you managed this," she said, openly admiring.

"The maître d' knows me. I've been here many times through the years."

She picked up the huge, glossy menu. "I see."

He tipped down her menu and frowned over the top of it. "Why that disapproving little voice?"

Wide-eyed, she feigned innocence. "I don't know what you mean."

He shook his head at her. "Yes, I've been here with other women. And business associates. And my father and sister."

"I wasn't prying," she said defensively.

"No, but you're a woman, and you wondered."

She dropped the menu on the table with a faint thump. "You seem very knowledgeable about women."

"I'm thirty-three, Debra." He sounded a trifle irritated.

She glared at him. "You're so darn sure of yourself!"

"Would you really want a man who wasn't?"

That made her think. "No," she said slowly, discovering something about herself she'd never realized before. "No, I wouldn't."

He took her hand in his and stroked her palm, then brought it to his lips and kissed her inner wrist. "Perhaps you're beginning to understand me, honey. Do you think that's possible?"

"Perhaps."

She eased her hand from his and lifted the menu, but the words danced before her eyes. She could still feel his lips on her wrist, and as a consequence, she couldn't think what to order. Fortunately Clint was now occupied with the wine list. When they both decided on lobster thermidor, he ordered a chardonnay and declined to order a cocktail for himself since she'd decided against one.

After he had given their order to the black-tuxedoed waiter, Clint lifted his wine glass.

"Here's to a memorable evening. One of many."

She smiled, reserving comment, and lifted her glass to clink it with his. Instead of smiling in response, Clint frowned and set down his glass.

"You're not willing to commit yourself even that far, are you, Debra?"

"I beg your pardon?" It wasn't pretense; she didn't know what he was driving at.

He sighed and shook his head. "I meant," he stressed, "that you didn't second it when I referred to our going out together in future."

"Let's see how tonight goes first, shall we?" She, too, set down her glass. "I want to enjoy this evening, Clint. I'm trying to put behind me our past misunderstandings, our past arguments."

"Such a cautious lady. Don't you ever jump in first and think afterward?"

Her brows knit. "Not with a man like you, I don't."

"A man like me? What's that supposed to mean?"

The waiter brought their salads just then, and the interruption allowed Debra time to consider her reply. Clint had a tight look about his mouth, and she longed to recapture the lighthearted mood they'd had in the car.

She forced a saucy smile. "Why, Clint, your own sister said you were a rogue with the ladies. I'm guarding my heart, that's all."

To her relief, laughter lines deepened around his lips and eyes. "I'll accept that excuse for now." His eyes met hers.

"We'll see how cautious you are later tonight." He speared a slice of tomato and swallowed it with relish.

After that he set out to entertain her with anecdotes of his many travels, never once alluding to anything serious. It was when he was recounting the time he had backpacked a hundred miles along the John Muir trail as far as Mount Whitney that he inquired if she had ever done any backpacking.

She swallowed a mouthful of lobster. "No, I haven't. I like the country, I suppose everyone does. But give me a spotless motel at night, not some flimsy tent or sleeping bag."

"No sleeping under the stars? You don't know what you're missing." He buttered a roll, then leaned across the table to whisper. "It can be quite romantic."

"I'll take your word for it," she said with a delicate shiver, even though the picture he drew had a certain appeal. "I'd be scared of snakes and cougars and other creepy crawlies. I'm a city girl, in case you haven't guessed." She laughed lightly.

"I can see that," he bantered. "I'll be happy to protect you against all those pesky predators."

"I'll bet. But who would protect me against you?"

He grinned. "No one, I hope."

She sipped her wine, then sent him a curious look. "At my house that day, you said you were a country boy. Where did you grow up?"

"Wisconsin. Dad had a farm there until I was about fifteen. It was a great place for a boy to grow up, but it was difficult for Dad to make much money. He skimped until he could buy a hardware store in town, then another small business. One acquisition followed another." He shrugged. "He's been very successful."

"But you missed the outdoors?"

His smile was pensive. "I still do. When traffic and crowds get to me, I head for the woods, literally."

"I can see you there," she said thoughtfully, "but not completely. You're too at ease handling the company while your father is gone."

He set down his knife and fork and waited until the busboy had cleared away their plates and the waiter had gone for the dessert trolley before he answered.

"We're all made up of many facets, aren't we? Sure, I like the outdoors, but I also enjoy the challenge of business. There are ten engineers in my company, all highly specialized in various fields. Right now we have a backlog of contracts that will keep us busy for the next two years. That's pretty good for a five-year-old enterprise."

"It certainly is," she agreed wholeheartedly.

Not once had Clint indicated any expectations regarding his father's company. She respected him for charting his own life, for gambling on his own success or failure. No matter what, he would make his own way. She had a hunch his success would, in time, surpass his father's. Still, she suspected a part of Clint would always yearn for the freedom of open spaces, and she could visualize his life being a combination of the two.

A woman who shared her life with a man who, despite financial success, retained his love of simple pleasures, would be fortunate indeed. She could see him taking his future children backpacking, nurturing in them his own love of the outdoors.

She felt a sudden ache within her. The picture of him with some faceless woman, in a family that did not include her, made her feel sad. Heaven's, now she was being silly—and fanciful. She dabbed her lips with her napkin. What an idiot she was, mooning over his life when she should be concentrating on her own.

Clint took her hand, and immediately she could feel her pulse doing double time. She liked the feel of her hand locked with his, but such actions threatened her composure. She would have pulled her hand away, but he held on.

"Would you like dessert?" He indicated the loaded cart that the waiter had brought.

"Goodness, I don't know where I'll put it, but I can't resist." She dithered over a chocolate eclair and strawberry tart, but finally chose the tart.

Clint, with a faint smile, chose the eclair, and the second the waiter had poured their coffees and left, Clint released her hand to cut his eclair in half. Without a word he set one half on the side of her dessert plate.

"Oh, I couldn't," she protested, though her mouth was already watering. "It's yours. I can't take it."

"Debra, I chose it for you."

She looked at him in surprise and felt her heart bump at the warmth in his eyes. It was thoughtful of him, and she thanked him, knowing instinctively he'd be embarrassed if she made too much of his gesture.

"You must think I'm dreadfully greedy, but I love sweets." She sampled the eclair and uttered a sound of sheer bliss. "I deserve to be fat."

Clint sipped his coffee and watched her over the rim of his cup, his dessert untouched. "You'll never be fat. You know what they say, if you want to know how your girl will look twenty years from now, take a look at her mother. And your mother is still a very attractive lady."

She stirred sugar and cream into her coffee. Clint, she noticed, drank his black. "Mom is attractive, isn't she?"

He nodded, finally tasting his eclair. "Has she ever thought of marrying again?"

"Oh no!" The reply sprang from Debra, then seeing the penetrating look Clint sent her, she hastened to explain.

"Don't misunderstand." She spread her hands. "Much as I loved my father, I know Mom is often lonely. When I was in my teens and someone said to me what you've just said, I was outraged." She made a face. "Selfish little brat, that's what I was. But I idolized Dad and couldn't understand Mom ever wanting anyone else."

"You were a child then," Clint pointed out softly. "How would you feel about it now?"

"I'd be happy for her," she said in all sincerity. "But I don't think it will happen." She sat back. "Mom is, I think, a one-man woman."

"And you, Debra, are you a one-man woman?"

She picked up her fork and attacked the last piece of her tart. "How should I know?"

"Then Brian wasn't the man?"

"Lord no!"

"I'm glad to have my opinion confirmed."

She looked at him, her fork poised in midair. "Feeling vindicated, are you, that it was pride, not my heart, that was broken?"

"It's always encouraging for a man when he makes the right guesses about a woman."

"But you have such extensive experience. It shouldn't be any problem for you."

"Not challenging me again, are you?"

She shook her head. "No."

By now she knew it would be dangerous to issue anything resembling a dare to Clint. It disconcerted her that he had correctly assessed her, while she still felt unsure of him. Although she had learned more about his background, it had only served to strengthen her belief that she was the vulnerable one, not Clint. This man could hurt her, and hurt her more than Brian had.

It was a shattering thought, and once again it occurred to her that maybe her earlier instincts had been right after all. She shouldn't have come out with Clint. She should have continued to do what he had accused her of that day at the reception; she should have run in the opposite direction.

"You have a pretty face and a quite exquisite body, Debra, but I do prefer your mind present when we're together."

Her gaze flew to his. "Sorry, was I daydreaming again?"

"It would seem so." He dropped some bills in the leather folder the waiter had left on the table. "I wish I knew what you were thinking when you get that troubled look on your face."

"Troubled? I'm not troubled." She lowered her eyes and gathered up her sweater and purse. "You've just fed me, remember? I'm never troubled on a full stomach."

He rose and pulled back her chair as she got to her feet. "Then why do I get this feeling you've left me, mentally?"

"I have no idea."

She was conscious of him walking at her back, and once they left the confines of the dining tables, he moved to her side, his hand possessive on her waist.

"You're not being truthful, Debra." His eyes were serious as he looked down at her. "I wonder what it will take to make you trust me?" he murmured as they passed through the crowded cocktail lounge.

She waited until they were outdoors before answering.

"I'm a modern woman," she tossed up at him with a brash smile. "I don't trust any man."

"Then it's time you did." His tone was sharp and his touch ungentle when he pulled her sweater from where it lay over her arm. He spread the sweater over her shoulders, letting his hands linger. "Why do you pretend to be hard and uncaring?"

The night air was cool, and Clint's remark made her feel colder still. "Maybe I am hard and uncaring," she snapped, disliking intensely that description of herself.

"Nonsense." His fingers tightened on her shoulders, and he urged her into the Lincoln. "It's a defense mechanism." He walked to the driver's side, slid in and turned to her before starting the engine. "You've been hurt." He stroked her cheek, tipped her chin and leaned over to kiss her tenderly on the lips. It was a fleeting, feathery kiss; a kiss meant to comfort, not to instill passion.

She pulled away, even though she savored the feeling of his lips on hers. She didn't know what she wanted exactly, she just knew she was fed up with kisses that insinuated at hidden fires that were never, it appeared, to be ignited.

Blue eyes glinted, first with surprise, then swift temper at her rejection. "What's bothering you now?" he asked, sounding every bit as fed up as she felt.

"Nothing."

He sighed. "Now why don't I believe you?"

His question, as far as she was concerned, required no answer. She could feel him looking at her and trying to gauge her mood. He pushed up the armrest and leaned closer. Gently he threaded his fingers through her hair and wrapped a strand around his forefinger.

"Your hair feels like silk," he whispered, all signs of his early impatience with her gone.

Again she eased toward the door until the handle jabbed into her hip. Clint's wide shoulders blocked off the lights from the parking lot, and the noise of cars arriving and leaving seemed to come from afar. Much as a part of her wanted this slow seduction of the senses to go on forever, another part of her screamed caution.

Clint noticed the slight withdrawal and misread it. The sensuous curve of his mouth hardened. "You needn't flinch away. I gave up making out in a car a long, long time ago, Red."

"I'm glad to hear it." Her tongue moistened her lower lip.

He groaned softly and reached for her. His hand slid around her back, pulling her toward him. In the next instant his mouth claimed hers, and with a soft sigh she melted against him, no longer trying to find reasons to resist him. Instead she kissed him back and shuddered uncontrollably when he parted her lips with his.

She felt bemused and was aware only of strong arms holding her, of lips that tantalized hers, of hands that caressed her and sought the softness of her curves through the thin fabric of her dress. But when his finger traced along the deep scoop of her neckline she wriggled away, even while craving the intimacy.

He lifted his head from where he'd been kissing the side of her neck and looked down at her, smiling at her in a way that made the blood rush through her.

"That's going to have to hold us for a while, honey," he drawled slowly as his hands slipped to her waist.

He moved to his side of the car, but his eyes reflected a banked down hunger, and she knew it had taken willpower for him to release her. Now that she wasn't cocooned in his embrace she felt chilled, and despaired to find her hands shaking as she drew her sweater around her.

"I—I think that's more than enough." She readjusted the armrest, setting up that tiny barricade, conscious all the while of Clint watching her, a faint smile on his mouth.

"No, it isn't, sweetheart. It's not enough for you, and it's certainly not enough for me."

Chapter Six

For those moments in Clint's arms, Debra had been aware of nothing but him and the response he stirred within her. Now it came as a jolt to see car lights flashing in the parking lot and to hear patrons speaking in small convivial groups as they left the restaurant.

She glanced at the clock on the illuminated dash as Clint drove into the street. It was ten o'clock, only three hours since Clint had called for her, but she felt far removed from the woman who had looked forward to this evening with both anticipation and apprehension.

Clint was no longer quite the mystery he had been, but such knowledge, however interesting, had seemed of little importance when he took her in his arms. The outside world, with its sensible questions and answers, had faded to insignificance.

Scary, that's what it was, to learn that a few moments in a man's arms could drive rational thought from her mind. Scary to learn she could lose herself to the extent that nothing was more important than having him hold her again.

She glanced over at Clint. He'd been silent, as had she, since leaving the restaurant. Perhaps he was also mulling over the happenings of this evening. He must have felt her looking at him because he turned his head toward her and smiled. Taking one hand off the wheel for a second, he squeezed her hand, something he had done before on occasion. That brief gesture made her feel good inside, as if she mattered to him.

If she were truthful, she would admit that she liked the deference Clint had shown her all evening, a deference accorded her because she was a woman. This courtliness had come as something of a surprise. He was, after all, a modern and dynamic man. She couldn't remember any other man treating her in quite the same way, and independent though she was, she had enjoyed being treated like delicate porcelain.

Then why did she feel this trepidation? Why did she feel she must fight this overwhelming attraction she felt for him? After all, Clint was someone both men and women could respect and admire: a loyal son, a loving brother, a lover of nature and a most attentive escort. She ticked off his attributes one by one, but nothing could allay her sense of danger.

She expected Clint to take her straight home, but instead he turned off the main highway when they reached Corona del Mar and drove down a palm-lined street to park his car overlooking the ocean.

"Like a walk?" He nodded towards the lawns and path skirting the top of the bluff. The sound of waves was discernible even through the closed windows of the car.

"I'd love to," she agreed, noticing another couple strolling along the path, both of them wearing warm sweaters and slacks. "I could do with some exercise after that meal."

"Will you be warm enough?" Clint asked as they stepped from the car, his glance taking in her thin dress and light sweater.

"I'll be fine. I would really enjoy a walk."

Lines creased his forehead, and before she realized what he was doing, he had removed his suit jacket and wrapped it around her, surrounding her in his warmth and male scent.

He rubbed her arm to stimulate its circulation. "Does that feel better?"

Even through the fine wool she could feel an electric charge shoot clear through her at the contact. "Much better," she replied huskily, "but what about you?"

"Don't worry about me. I come from the cold north, remember? You probably feel the cold more than I do." He started along the path, his arm still around her.

She tipped back her head to look up at him. "You're a considerate man, aren't you?"

As she might have expected, he seemed embarrassed by her compliment, but she felt he was pleased, too. She had meant what she had said, and was glad she had voiced her appreciation.

"Well, now, my mother would have been happy to hear you say that," he told her with a faint smile. "Mom was a firm believer in the golden rule of treating others as you want to be treated."

"You can't go wrong with trying to live up to that," Debra agreed solemnly. "Do you know, that's the first time you've mentioned your mother?"

"Is it? Strange, because Mom and I were close. She hated leaving the land, too, but worked right along with Dad to build up his business. They were a team." He sighed heavily. "I wish she was alive today to see how successful Dad's been." Clint frowned and looked down at her. "Hey, how did we get so serious?"

"I don't know," she whispered.

After that, as if by mutual consent, they fell silent, walking side by side, murmuring "good evening" whenever they passed another couple. When Clint paused to stare down at the incessantly rolling waves, Debra, content, leaned her head against his shoulder and watched the moonlight sparkling on the white, foamy crests curling toward the shore.

She breathed in the fresh, damp air and huddled closer to Clint. She'd been warm enough while they were walking, but now that they were standing still, the ocean mist was seeping into her bones.

Clint must have felt her shiver, for he looked down at her snuggled against his side. Without a word he turned her about, and they headed along the path toward the car. Once inside, he didn't start the engine right away, and she was surprised to see strain etching lines at the corners of his mouth.

"My house is near here." He looked her straight in the eyes. "Will you come there with me?"

"Now?"

"Yes, now." He sounded impatient, but whether with himself or her, she wasn't sure.

She lowered her lashes and slipped off his jacket. Without speaking, he helped her and donned the jacket himself.

"Well?" he demanded.

More than anything else, she wanted to be held close to him again, but asking her to his house made it obvious he wouldn't be satisfied with a few kisses.

"No." Surprisingly, her voice was steady.

"I knew you'd refuse." He sounded so disgruntled that despite her inner storm, she found her lips twitching. When his eyes took on the wicked glint with which she was becoming familiar, she knew he had seen that tentative grin. "I can see I haven't used enough persuasion," he drawled.

"You'd be wasting your time." She was determined to keep things light, and hoped fervently that Clint would never guess what her refusal had cost her.

"I wonder." He started the car and drew away from the curb. "Perhaps now I'm being too considerate. A woman doesn't always say what she means."

His remark annoyed her. "This one does. Don't let your experience with women fool you. We aren't all alike. We're individuals."

"I'm well aware of that, Debra, so don't get huffy. But no matter what anyone says, I believe men and women still have some basic differences. A true man will always be the hunter rather than the hunted, and except for the more aggressive female, I think most women like it that way."

"Really? And what characteristics make up the true woman, may I ask?"

He gave her a hooded look. "Oh no you don't. I'm not falling into that trap. I'm not generalizing about women. If I keep one step ahead of you, I'll consider myself damn lucky."

She managed a careless laugh. "Now who's being cautious? I think I'll consider I've won this round."

"You think what you like, honey. I prefer it when my opponent gets overconfident."

"I'm not overconfident." She assumed an expression of playful sternness and hoped it masked how churned up she felt. "I intend keeping one step ahead of you, Clint Rasmussen. Maybe several!"

"Hmm, I wonder who'll win?" he asked softly. "Maybe we'll both get what we want."

Debra gave him a quick look, wondering what he meant, but he was watching the traffic, a faint smile still on his lips. With her back cradled against the plush gray upholstery and a dreamy ballad playing on the tape deck, she should feel comfortable. But Clint's invitation had destroyed any thought of relaxation. She couldn't believe it, but for a few charged moments she had been tempted.

Tempted to experience the unknown, perhaps? No! The silent question both startled and dismayed her. Lord, Clint had warned her he preferred being the hunter rather than the hunted. It was up to her to see that she was not an easy prey.

Silent warnings to herself in no way lessened her expectation as they walked up the darkened path to her town house some twenty minutes later. Clint's arm was around her waist. The light from the street lamp eluded the individual entryways of the homes, and she had to rummage blindly in her small purse to find her key. Her nervousness increased as she fumbled, and she wished Clint would say something light and easy, now when she needed it. She was relieved when she got the door open and light from a lamp in the living room filtered through to the front entryway. Only then did she face Clint.

"Thank you for a terrific evening, Clint. I really enjoyed myself." She was appalled that nerves made her thank-you sound perfunctory, her sincerity nullified.

"My pleasure."

His deep voice was faintly mocking, and Debra had the distinct impression he knew she was keyed up. Still, his slow smile made short work of any annoyance she might have felt at his correct interpretation of her mood. As she expected, and perhaps had unconsciously counted upon,

he wasn't being put off by any stilted thank-you. She made
no pretense of dissuading him from entering the town
house with her, accepting that as inevitable.

Her heart thumped when she heard the decisive click of
the front door a second before he followed her into the
living room. In an attempt to appear composed, she tossed
her purse and sweater on a chair, then turned to ask,
"Would you like some coffee, or a liqueur?" She crossed
to the buffet in the adjacent dining area where a small col-
lection of bottles and glasses were set out on a tray. "We
have Kahlua or crème de menthe."

"A little Kahlua will be fine," he said.

Her hand was unsteady when she handed him his liqueur
glass, especially when she noticed he had loosened his tie
and removed his jacket.

"Aren't you having any?" he asked as they sat on the
sofa. When she shook her head, he made no comment.
Instead he sipped his drink, savoring the taste, then set his
glass on the cocktail table and turned to rest his arm along
the sofa at her back. "You know, we've managed a whole
evening without any serious disagreement." He leaned
closer, his lips hovering over hers so she could smell the
coffee scent of the Kahlua and feel the warmth of his
breath on her cheek. "Fighting is such a waste of time,"
he murmured, his lips teasing hers. "This is more pleasant, don't you think?"

He had lifted his head, as if waiting for an answer, and
somehow she managed one. "Yes, yes it is," she whispered, excitement burgeoning inside her. Certain that in
her own home she had some control over his actions, she
made no pretense of resistance as he drew her into his
arms.

She raised her face to his and traced the scar through his
brow with her fingertip. "How did this happen?" She was

purposely delaying the kiss she knew was coming, trying to appear nonchalant, or at least as self-possessed as he was.

"Hockey." His hand on her shoulder tightened, and the one on her waist began to caress her.

"I thought it would be some rough contact sport," she told him with an impish grin, though her voice was breathless.

"You did, did you?" On a half laugh, he reached behind her and turned off the lamp, plunging them into darkness, except for a sliver of moonlight penetrating the drapes.

And then there was no more time for delaying tactics. His mouth was on hers, gently coaxing; and with a sigh she lifted her arms to his shoulders, cupping the back of his neck with one hand and giving herself up to his sweet seduction. A delicious lethargy swept over her, and she was hardly aware of him lifting her onto his lap until she was lying cradled across his legs. Her position made her feel vulnerable, but it didn't seem to matter. Her breath caught in her throat as he kissed the soft skin of her neck and nibbled at her earlobe.

"God, you're lovely," he whispered against her skin, his hands roaming over her curves, spreading fire wherever they touched. Feminine caution made her clasp his hand and murmur a husky, "Don't!" in his ear. He groaned softly but accepted the limits she set. His lips returned to hers.

But this time he was not coaxing a response from her; this time he was demanding it. Perhaps his passion had been aroused by those brief caresses, perhaps her protest had aroused the hunter deep within him. Whichever it was, the hunter was definitely in control. Even while she still had enough presence of mind to realize what was happening, the flames whipping through her veins made resistance impossible. A soft cry of protest emitted against the mouth possessing hers, but at the same time she released her hold on his hand and lifted both arms to his shoulders, where her fingers caressed the crisp hair at his nape.

She felt him shudder against her, and her own body trembled when he cajoled her lips apart, their breaths mingling in a kiss of such intimacy it rocked her to her very core. For an instant she tried to draw away, but Clint softened his lips against hers, seducing her until their kisses took on a kind of frenzy, and the darkened room filled with the sound of their breathing and the faint rustle of their movements.

Now when Clint's hand stroked beneath first one and then the other of the swelling curves that seemed to entice him so, her sharply indrawn breath had nothing to do with protest. She could feel the warmth of his fingers through her thin bodice. Lost in the euphoria of sensations she'd never before experienced, she was only vaguely aware of the slight tug on the zipper of her dress, her satisfied moan echoing Clint's as the loosened dress enabled him to seek the softness of her flesh.

"Oh, Clint," she cried softly as he touched her beneath the wisp of a bra. Her limbs felt lax and pliable, and she instinctively lifted herself to make it easier for him to release the bra snap at her back. With nothing impeding him, he caressed her, his breath warm as he kissed that sensitive part of her.

And suddenly, shockingly, it wasn't enough. Debra loosened a button of his shirt and slipped her hand inside. She could feel the steady beat of his heart beneath her palm as her fingertips stroked the hair-roughened skin, but when he deepened their kiss her fingers clenched involuntarily, tugging at the short crisp hairs, making him grunt. With a

PLAY
SILHOUETTE'S

LUCKY HEARTS
GAME

AND YOU COULD GET

★ FREE BOOKS
★ A FREE CLOCK/CALENDAR
★ A FREE SURPRISE GIFT
★ AND MUCH MORE

TURN THE PAGE AND
DEAL YOURSELF IN →

PLAY "LUCKY HEARTS" AND YOU COULD GET...

★ Exciting Silhouette Romance™ novels—FREE
★ A Lucite Clock/Calendar—FREE
★ A surprise mystery gift that will delight you—FREE

THEN CONTINUE YOUR LUCKY STREAK WITH A SWEETHEART OF A DEAL

When you return the postcard on the opposite page, we'll send you the books and gifts you qualify for, absolutely free! Then, you'll get 6 new Silhouette Romance novels every month, delivered right to your door months before they're available in stores. If you decide to keep them, you'll pay only $1.95* per book and there is <u>no</u> charge for postage and handling! You can cancel at any time by marking "cancel" on your statement or returning a shipment to us at our cost.

★ Free Newsletter!
You'll get a free newsletter—an insider's look at our most popular authors and their upcoming novels.

★ Special Extras—Free!
When you subscribe to Silhouette Books, you'll also get additional free gifts from time to time as a token of our appreciation for being a home subscriber.

*Terms and prices subject to change.

DETACH AND MAIL CARD TODAY

SILHOUETTE "NO RISK" GUARANTEE

★ You're not required to buy a single book—ever!
★ As a subscriber, you must be completely satisfied or you may cancel at any time by marking "cancel" on your statement or returning a shipment of books to us at our cost.
★ The free books and gifts you receive from this LUCKY HEARTS offer remain yours to keep—in any case.

If offer card is missing, write to:
Silhouette Books, 901 Fuhrmann Blvd., P.O. Box 1867, Buffalo, NY 14269-1867

BUSINESS REPLY CARD

First Class   Permit No. 717   Buffalo, NY

Postage will be paid by addressee

Silhouette Reader Service
901 Fuhrmann Blvd.
P.O. Box 1867
Buffalo, NY 14240-9952

NO POSTAGE
NECESSARY
IF MAILED
IN THE
UNITED STATES

deft turn he pulled her around until they were both lying full-length on the sofa.

"You're everything any man could want," he murmured, bending over her and kissing her hard on the mouth.

"Clint, I don't think..."

Whatever she'd been going to say was muffled by another kiss, this one gentler and therefore far more seductive. Her alarm at finding herself lying beside him was swamped by a yearning too powerful to resist. She trembled in his arms, half frightened, half eager. Immediately she felt herself drawn closer to him, felt the hairs on his chest tickling her skin, the sensation an aphrodisiac. She moaned against his lips, conscious of the tightening of his hold on her, of the hard muscled length of him against her soft feminine shape.

Soon his slow kisses and provocative caresses over her bared skin drove all thought from her mind. The taste and touch of him filled her very being. Nothing else mattered but this closeness, this feeling of rightness. She whimpered when he tugged her hand from around his neck and inched away from her, as much as was possible on the narrow sofa. No longer held against his warmth, she felt the cool air on her breasts. Instinctively she reached for him, wanting to cuddle against him again.

"No, love," he murmured with obvious regret as he held her away from him. "We have to stop now, or there'll be no stopping."

"But..." She shook her head, trying to clear it, and crossed her arms over her bared breasts. Her trance of seconds ago, where nothing and no one existed but Clint and the response he aroused within her, was slowly but surely ebbing, leaving her with a sick feeling of emptiness.

"I knew I should have insisted we go back to my place."
His lips brushed across her forehead. "When I take you to
bed, sweetheart, I want all night long. I don't want to
worry about your mother or anyone else walking in on us."

She gasped, the thought of her mother coming in and
finding her half-naked in his arms acting like a torrent of
cold water on her overheated flesh. But it was his pre-
sumption that it was a foregone conclusion he would take
her to bed eventually that drove her to push against his
chest, and push hard.

"You take too much for granted," she protested in a
thin, wavering voice, not sounding in the least as she had
intended. Instead of sounding indignant, she sounded uncertain.

He caught her hand and stroked her palm with his
thumb. "Do I?" There was that teasing note in his voice
that she found irresistible. "Oh, I don't think so, honey,
but I'm not fond of short sofas where my feet hang over
the edge. I picture us in my big roomy bed."

"Well, you can think again." Her tone was low, impassioned. "That is never, ever, going to happen!"

The sudden realization of how close she had come to
complete surrender made her squirm inwardly with shame.
She, too, could see the picture he drew, and with a clarity
that was earthshaking.

"You make it a habit to go this far and then stop, do
you?"

"No!" She could feel her face flame and thanked
heaven he couldn't see her expression.

"I'm glad to hear it. With most men, you'd be asking
for trouble."

She had a hysterical urge to laugh. Did he believe she
indulged in such scenes on a regular basis? If he only knew
the truth!

"You're the one who called the halt," she pointed out, then wished she could recall that reckless admission.

"True. But gentleman that I am, I wouldn't have reminded you of it."

The amusement in his voice annoyed her, and suddenly the incongruity of them lying side by side debating their actions struck her as ridiculous in the extreme.

"Will you get off this sofa?" She hadn't meant to sound quite so curt, but perhaps it was as well.

"Scared?" he taunted. He leaned over to kiss her, his lips finding her mouth unerringly, even in the dark. "Admit you wanted it to happen, and I'll do as you ask."

"My mother might come in!" she exclaimed, desperate and sounding it.

He laughed. "That sounds like something I used to hear when I was a teenager."

"Precocious, were you?" she retorted with a definite snap.

He swung his long legs over the edge of the sofa and leaned over and pulled her into a sitting position beside him.

"I'm the one who's aching like hell, honey, so I don't know why you're in a bad temper."

She felt hot all over at his dry sarcasm, but there was nothing she could say. Instead she scrambled to her feet and yanked at her dress, frantic to cover herself lest Clint should turn on the lamp. She was struggling with her back zipper when lamplight suddenly blinded her, making her blink.

"May I help?" Clint gestured at her zipper and moved toward her.

She stepped out of reach and bent her head. "No, I can manage."

When she did lift her head, it took every iota of courage to meet his gaze. He was tucking his shirt inside his slacks, but his eyes were on her, and had been, she suspected, from the instant he had turned on the lamp. She couldn't tell what he was thinking but found his steady gaze disconcerting.

"Why so nervous?" he asked, in what had become an uncomfortable silence.

"Isn't that obvious? You're the one who mentioned my mother could come in on us."

"That's not the only thing that's got you in a tizzy." He came toward her, and she curbed the impulse to step back. "What's wrong?" He laughed shortly. "You're acting like a teenager who's just fended off her first pass."

She stiffened. "I'm hardly a teenager!"

"True, and I doubt it's your first pass."

Furious eyes turned on him. "Nor the first one you've been guilty of, I'll bet."

He raised his hands, palms outstretched. "Look, I don't want to argue, but I object to your looking at me as if I've committed some crime. I didn't do anything you didn't want." He moved as if to take her into his arms, then quite obviously stopped himself. "Hell, Debra, you dated Brian for a year. Don't tell me he never touched you."

He never touched me as you've done! she felt like screaming but didn't. A proud anger took hold of her. Let Clint think what he wanted. He'd judged her; let him live with that judgment. She owed him no explanations. Anyway, by the look of distaste on his face, his suspicions brought him no satisfaction.

How could he think of Brian and her previous involvement with him, just minutes after they had...? She shook her head and fought down a sudden nausea.

Immersed in her thoughts, she gave a start when Clint's hands closed over her shoulders. Feeling wretched and confused, she neither pushed him away nor welcomed him. Instead she stared up at him, her eyes reflecting her hurt and bewilderment.

"Don't you know, can't you guess what's eating into me?" he demanded roughly, giving her a slight shake before pulling her close. "I can't bear the thought of him touching you, of any man touching you, except me. God, how I wish I could have been the first man in your life, the man who had the privilege of teaching you about love."

She almost succumbed then, almost told him the truth, but something held her back. It wouldn't do to reveal all her secrets to Clint. Already he was disrupting her very existence. At their first meeting she'd felt she could confide in him and had done so. But this was different. She'd known all along her attraction was strong for this man, but nothing had prepared her for the intensity of her response tonight. The reason for her susceptibility to him could only mean one thing, but right now she wasn't ready to accept the reason hovering in her subconscious.

"And would I be your first woman?" She couldn't believe she had asked that question, couldn't believe the acid flippancy of her tone. Instantly Clint's softened expression hardened to one that excluded her. "Don't worry, Clint, I'm not prying into your personal life." She stepped away from him. "I'd appreciate it if you would afford me the same courtesy."

"I'll try, but it won't be easy," he astounded her by retorting. "What we shared was special, Debra," he added on a different note. "We both know that, don't we?"

She looked away, anywhere but at Clint. He was demanding that she admit she shared his feeling, but she was too unsure of him for that, too unsure of her own mud-dled emotions, and too proud to admit to anything.

Clint rubbed the back of his neck, looking suddenly weary. "I guess I should have expected this," he mused. "Your experience with Brian has scared you from making any commitment to me."

"Why oh why must you keep harping about Brian?" she cried, exasperated.

"Because he still haunts you, that's why. I know he only hurt your pride, but isn't it time you got over it? Isn't it time you joined the living?"

"By that I suppose you mean when am I going to bed with you?" she accused, by now too distraught to be cir-cumspect.

Clint chuckled. "I admit I want that, and want it badly, but that's not what I'm speaking about." His hand slipped to her shoulder where he caressed her collarbone. "Most times we're together, I'm conscious that you're afraid to let yourself go, afraid to feel." He traced her lower lip with his forefinger. "But tonight, earlier on, I think you were as happy being with me as I was with you. Can you deny that?"

"I told you I enjoyed the evening," she reminded him impatiently.

"Well, then, if you can admit that, why can't you be honest about how you feel?" He inclined his head toward the sofa, his meaning plain.

She avoided his eyes. "What do you expect of me, Clint? What do you want me to say?"

"If I have to choose your words for you, Debra, they won't mean much to either one of us." He swung away from her and was already at the front door when he flung over his shoulder, "Perhaps I'm wrong. Perhaps all you do need for happiness is your pride."

Chapter Seven

Debra sank onto the sofa, her legs no longer any support, her mind resisting Clint's harsh condemnation. The instant he had walked out she had wanted to call him back. She couldn't remember ever feeling more alone, more heartsick.

How had it happened? More to the point, how had she allowed it to happen? For without her realizing it, that compelling physical attraction she'd felt for Clint right from their first meeting had turned into love.

Hardly aware of what she was doing, she got to her feet again and walked over to the stereo where she lifted her father's picture and stared down at it as if, in some way, that dear face could bring her solace.

"Was I wrong, Dad? Should I have admitted I cared?" She pressed the framed photograph to her chest. "I love him, Dad, and now I've driven him away."

But the smiling face, when she looked at it again, gave her no answers. She was on her own. For the first time she questioned whether she had followed her father's principles more literally than he may have intended. Still, she didn't want to make a fool of herself over Clint. Sighing, she set the photograph down, and leaving the light on for her mother, she went upstairs to bed.

What exactly did Clint mean when he said those moments were "special" to him, Debra wondered minutes later as she lay in bed. Did he mean she aroused him more than the other women he had known? She scowled at the darkened ceiling, the very thought repugnant. She longed for him to love her for what she was, with that volatile physical chemistry between them being a direct result of that love. If all he felt for her was desire, it just wasn't enough.

She rolled over and buried her head in her pillow. She dared not believe that he loved her. After all, he hadn't committed himself that far. But then, he must have found her reticence regarding her own feelings discouraging. In the circumstances, he would hardly have declared he was madly in love with her.

Her teeth dug into her lip. He had made the first overture. It wouldn't have hurt her to give him the tiniest hint that she cared. His subsequent reaction might have afforded her some clue as to the depth of his emotions.

Would he, then, have suggested an affair? Marriage? Her hands were shaking as she thumped her pillow. Marriage was probably the last thing on his mind. He'd been a freewheeling bachelor for a long time. Even his work required the mobility and spontaneity of a man who had no ties.

No, it was just as well she'd been discreet. If she'd learned nothing else from her experience with Brian, she'd learned she had to control her tendency to be too trusting. She couldn't afford to be gullible again.

Besides, she'd been brought up with some old-fashioned values. If a man loved you, really loved you, he declared that love and proposed marriage. For her, anything less would only lead to misery, because she would doubt his sincerity.

"You're out of touch with the times, woman," she muttered with a last thump of her pillow. She fell asleep with the memory of Clint's blue eyes staring at her with accusation and regret.

At breakfast next morning, her mother's questions about her date with Clint proved difficult to answer. Debra knew by her mother's slight frown that she guessed something was amiss.

"I suppose you wondered why I changed my bridge night," Marilyn said in what appeared to be a change of subject.

With all that had happened, Debra had forgotten about her mother's change of schedule. She nodded, curious as to why her mother looked ill at ease.

"I decided I shouldn't always be here when you came home with a man," Marilyn confessed. "I suggested to the others that we play last night." She concentrated on spreading jam on her toast. "I realize a mother's presence, even if she is upstairs in bed, may be inhibiting."

"It's your home, Mom, and any man dating me will have to accept that, or he needn't bother asking me out." Debra paused in the act of sugaring her coffee. "Come to think of it, you never did a disappearing act when I was dating Brian. What are you up to, Mother?"

"You shouldn't be suspicious of your mother, young lady."

Debra set her spoon on her saucer. "Mother, you aren't matchmaking, are you?" she asked with a disapproving shake of her head.

"And why not?" her mother replied defensively. "I like Clint. He may have made you angry at the wedding, but whether you admit it or not, he was kind to you, and caring about his sister. What's more, last night he lived up to my expectations."

"In what way?"

"He isn't like the other men you've dated, who make it obvious they're bored talking with your mother. He showed real interest in your growing up years and spoke about his parents and sister with affection."

Debra's brows drew together. "I hope you didn't tell him too much about me."

"Are you afraid he may get behind your defenses?" Marilyn's gaze was thoughtful. "Clint reminds me of your father, Debra." When Debra showed her surprise, her mother hurried on. "Not in looks, dear, but in strength. A woman could depend on him. He's not one of those weak types who's only too pleased to have a woman shoulder all the responsibilities."

"That's rather a snap judgment, isn't it, after a first meeting?" Debra sipped her coffee. It was strange, really, that both she and her mother should come to the same opinion.

"I've learned to trust my first impressions," Marilyn replied quietly.

Debra heaved a sigh. "I wish I could." She set down her cup and started to clear the dishes from the breakfast bar. "Brian fooled me completely."

"You were blinded by his looks. We learn by our mistakes, dear, even if it is painful."

"I guess so," Debra conceded, turning to rinse the dishes before putting them in the dishwasher.

"I don't know what occurred between you and Clint to make you look so unhappy this morning," her mother said from behind her, "and believe me, I'm not prying. Just remember, his type doesn't come along often."

Before Debra could reply, her mother left the kitchen and went upstairs. Debra might have poured out her troubles to her mother had she remained a moment longer, but now she was glad she hadn't. There was little point in discussing Clint further. In all probability her offhandedness had ended any chance of his asking her out again.

Nevertheless, all day Saturday Debra jumped every time the phone rang, and the intensity of her disappointment when it wasn't Clint swamped her with wretchedness. If Clint allowed one setback to turn him off, then he couldn't love her. For once, she'd exercised good judgment. What if she'd admitted she loved him, only to have him ignore her afterward?

Then again, was she expecting too much? After all, she'd see him at the office. Maybe he felt there was no need to phone her. He couldn't know she was miserable and longed to hear his voice.

By Sunday evening, with still no phone call from Clint, she couldn't find much satisfaction in the fact that by hiding her feelings from him she had at least maintained her pride.

She was about to go to bed when the doorbell pierced the late evening quiet. Her heart leaped, yet cautious in case it was a stranger, she left the chain on the hook as she peered through the opening.

"Laurie!" she exclaimed with surprise. Controlling her disappointment that it wasn't Clint, Debra hastily unlatched the door.

"May I come in?" Laurie asked formally, her chin uplifted, her red-rimmed blue eyes hostile.

"Of course!"

Debra stepped aside, wondering frantically why Laurie was there, and why she was looking at her with such dislike. She guided the younger girl into the living room, but when Debra gestured for her to sit down, Laurie gave a curt shake of her head, her lips tight, her face drawn.

"Brian says you and he are in love," Laurie announced without preamble, the sudden trembling of her lips softening her earlier look of aggression.

"No!" Shocked, Debra stretched out her hands to the other girl, instinctively wanting to alleviate Laurie's obvious pain. "No, that's not true!" she reiterated with emphasis.

But Laurie wasn't about to accept her offer of comfort apparently, for she stepped out of reach.

"You can't deny you were dating Brian before he married me," Laurie accused, both her hands clutching the strap of her shoulder bag as if she needed something to cling to.

Debra ignored Laurie's belligerent pose and took her gently by the elbow. "Sit down, please." It was obvious to her that Laurie was putting up a valiant fight to ward off tears. "You're upset, and you have no need to be."

Despite the touch of hysteria in Laurie's tone, Debra managed to get her to sit down while she took the seat facing her.

"Yes, I dated Brian," Debra told the distraught girl reluctantly, "and maybe, for a time, we thought we were in love, but that's over and has been for quite a while."

Laurie sniffed and groped for a Kleenex. "We've had an awful fight," she mumbled. "He told me all about you."

What had Brian said, for goodness' sake, to get her in such a state, Debra thought angrily.

"Brian made his choice, and it was you," Debra pointed out gently. "You have nothing to fear from me, Laurie, honestly."

Her sincerity must have got through to Laurie, for her face lost its youthful defiance. She looked down at her hands and asked in a subdued voice, "Then you aren't in love with him?"

"No, I am not."

Laurie looked up, and instead of appearing relieved as Debra had expected, her face seemed to crumble.

"I don't think I am either," she wailed. "I've made a terrible mistake!"

"Oh, Laurie!" Debra rushed to her side and sat on the arm of Laurie's chair in order to put her arm across the weeping girl's shoulders. "What's wrong? Tell me, I want to help."

Laurie wiped her face childishly with the back of her hands. "We've done nothing but argue, and . . . and he looks at other women all the time!"

Damn Brian! It was one habit that had annoyed her as well, but somehow she had to comfort Laurie. "All men look at pretty girls," Debra said with a brightness she didn't feel.

"It isn't just that," Laurie protested vehemently. "Marriage isn't at all what I expected! I'm so miserable!" More tears ran down her face.

Debra hugged the younger girl to her, her recently acquired understanding of Brian's nature increasing her concern for Laurie. "My goodness, you've been married less than a month. It takes time to adjust, I'm sure," she said in an attempt to soothe. "It's far too soon to think you've made a mistake."

"Maybe." Laurie got to her feet and started pacing the room. "Oh, what should I do?" she burst out finally, looking at Debra with the helpless appeal of a hurt and pampered child.

"Surely you could talk to your father or brother," Debra suggested tentatively, uneasy in this new role as advisor to the lovelorn, especially when she felt so ill-qualified for the task.

"No, no!" Laurie cried and waved her hands in agitation. "That's the last thing I want! I know what they'll say. They'll say 'I told you so,' and I don't want to hear it!"

"But—"

"Debra, promise me you won't tell Clint!"

"I'd never discuss your personal business with anyone, unless I had your permission to do so," Debra hastened to reassure her, "but I think you're being foolish. Clint and your father love you, they'll want to help."

Laurie tossed her blond head, her pretty face mulish. "I'll make my own decisions."

Debra tactfully refrained from pointing out that Laurie had sought her advice, that the dilemma Laurie was in was a direct result of her making her own decision and ignoring the advice of her father and brother. She was thankful, though, that Laurie had come to her, that in so doing she'd been able to relieve Laurie of any suspicions Brian had aroused.

And when Laurie was leaving, the younger girl turned to her with a friendly, if wavery, smile on her face. "Thanks for listening to me. I came here tonight feeling terrible, and I know I was hateful at first. I don't know why you've been so nice, but I do appreciate it."

Debra returned the smile, then frowned worriedly. "I still think you should confide in Clint or your father when he returns."

"No way!" Laurie gave her a quick, anxious look. "Remember, you promised, Debra!"

"I'll remember," Debra replied with misgivings. Then she closed the front door as Laurie disappeared down the path.

When Debra walked into the executive office on Monday, she was dreading her meeting with Clint—the first after their cool parting. As well, she had the added weight of Laurie's secret to contend with. Still, she prided herself that she looked composed in her summery tan-colored suit and crisp white blouse, with her hair swept up on top of her head and large gold hoop earrings her only jewelry. No one, she was certain, would ever guess from her outward appearance at the turmoil attacking her insides.

No one, that is, except Clint. She knew it the instant she knocked on his door and entered his office at his quiet command. Wearing a dark brown business suit, he stood by the window, looking out at the gray sky that had streamers of sunlight breaking through the haze. Debra's tension exaggerated the muted whirring of the sprinklers outdoors and the crunch of tires as employees arrived and parked their cars. Clint turned as she crossed the room, and acknowledged her cool greeting with a smile that was sardonic.

"Amazing," he drawled, "how you manage to don that cold, untouchable image."

"Clint—" she hurriedly flipped his desk calendar to the current date "—we have to ignore our personal relationship while at the office." She tried to sound businesslike.

"Is that what we have? A personal relationship?"

His tone mocked the notion, and she was flummoxed, unable to reply without becoming embroiled in a discussion she wanted to avoid. She couldn't function as his secretary while emotions cluttered her effectiveness. Why couldn't he see that? She frowned. Maybe he could and was choosing to be awkward.

His smile, such as it was, faded. "Debra, why do you always fight your instincts?"

"That's not true," she protested, unwilling to accept his allegation.

"I think you do." He shook his head at her. "I've thought about us a lot this weekend. When I left Friday night, I told myself I was a fool trying to break down the barriers you persist in raising between us." He paid no heed to her immediate objection and skirted the desk to come and stand before her, not touching her, but looking down into her eyes, mesmerizing her. "I've tried taking it slow with you, Debra, but I'll be here only a few more weeks. I have to attend to my own company."

She felt her heart sink; a terrible despair overwhelmed her. Whether what she was feeling was reflected on her face, she didn't know. But she couldn't—and wouldn't—express her feelings, and only continued to stare up at him and wonder how she could bear life without him.

His hands settled loosely on her waist, not drawing her closer, but she trembled at his touch nonetheless.

"I don't intend to let what we could have together slip by us, Debra." His lips brushed her cheek. "I'm laying siege, sweetheart, so don't fight me, okay?"

"No, no, I won't fight you," she whispered, happy for a second chance.

He groaned, and his arms tightened around her. "Don't look at me like that, sweetheart."

"I—I—" She swallowed, unable to go on, her heart full. Clint wasn't giving up on her, and she'd indicated her willingness. Gently she pressed her hands against his chest. "I—I have to get to work," she murmured at last.

He released her with obvious reluctance. "You're right, I suppose," he admitted with a heavy sigh.

She touched his cheek. "I'm glad we've made up." Her voice was soft as she made that concession—a concession she wouldn't have made in the recent past.

"I am, too, sweetheart. I am, too."

She looked up at him, her heart thudding, but she made herself turn away and hurry from his office. Minutes later, when she sat at her desk, she felt a certain satisfaction that their relationship had been reestablished without any real diminishing of her pride, although that hadn't been on her mind at the time—not at all.

And, thankfully, there had been no mention of Laurie. She hadn't had to feel guilty at the knowledge Laurie had entrusted to her, and that she had kept from Clint.

Debra stared dreamily across the elegant office, with its oil paintings on the walls, its deep easy chairs, the latest business magazines reposing on a huge square cocktail table. It took willpower to turn her attention to the report Clint must have put on her desk earlier. As she zipped paper into the typewriter and read the instructions he had written, she wondered when he'd had time to compile such a lengthy report. Perhaps while she had been imagining him bringing some beautiful woman home this weekend, he had instead been working. The thought reaffirmed the hope she was beginning to feel for their relationship, and she set to work with enthusiasm.

Before she knew it, it was lunchtime. Clint had spent a good part of the morning on the phone. When he opened his door and stopped by her desk, she looked up expectantly, feeling such a surge of love for him that she was shaken.

His smile filled her with a warm glow. "I'd hoped we could have lunch together," he told her, "but something has come up I have to attend to. I'm sorry."

She hid her disappointment. "Well, at the office, business must come first," she returned lightly.

He raised one brow in mute reminder of the times they had forgotten that rule. She felt her face grow warm, and frowned at him.

"Don't look cross," he said. "It's refreshing to know there are still women who can blush."

"I do not blush!"

"You do, and I like it." He leaned his knuckles on her desk. "But I like a lot of things about you," he murmured, "so we'll have dinner tonight, shall we?" His gaze slid over her.

She shuffled some papers on her desk. "I'd like that." She could almost feel his lips on hers. It was hard to suppress the longing to run her fingers through the crispness of his blond hair.

He straightened. "Good." He glanced at his watch. "I'll be back around two."

She watched him walk away, a tall, slim-hipped, powerfully shouldered man, and could feel that familiar yearning within her. Then some of the excitement she'd felt earlier faded. She didn't want her emotions controlled by the emotions and actions of another, but there didn't seem to be much she could do to stop falling in love. Clint was becoming the most important person in her life, and it frightened her. It gave him a power over her she didn't want anyone to possess.

Lunch in the cafeteria with Sharon pushed such doubts to the background. Sharon's suspected pregnancy had been confirmed by her doctor, and her joy proved contagious. For that brief hour it was Sharon's happy news, not

Debra's secret worries, that dominated their conversation.

But the instant Debra returned to her office, thoughts of Clint flooded through her, and with them the questions still unanswered. She plowed into the remainder of his long report, glad for the diversion and the chance to prove her accuracy. No matter that his reasons for her promotion had little to do with her capabilities, she was determined he should have no complaints. He had afforded her this opportunity, and she fully intended to earn his respect for her efficiency.

At five past two, Clint walked in with two men. "Any phone calls?" he asked by way of greeting, and accepted the yellow message slips she handed him. He glanced over them. "These can wait," he said, handing them back to her. Then he turned to his companions. "Come in, please," he said, opening the door to his office, "and let's see if we can reach some agreement on that contract." He glanced back at Debra as he was closing the door. "Hold my calls, please, Debra."

She almost laughed aloud when, with his face hidden from the other two men, he sent her the most outrageous wink. Somehow she kept a straight face.

"Certainly, Mr. Rasmussen," she returned primly.

An hour later she was engrossed in proofing the finished report, when a voice she hadn't heard for two weeks, and had no desire to hear, broke into her concentration.

"Hello, Debra." Brian half sat on the corner of her desk. "Congratulations on the promotion."

The first thing that occurred to her as she looked into Brian's too-even features was that no vestige of her infatuation remained. That practiced smile was meant to enthrall her, no doubt, but her heart maintained its steady beat. The relief was incredible. So much so that she could overlook the suggestiveness of his tone and the hint of a smirk in his brown eyes. Perfectly composed, she set Clint's report aside, ready to give to him when he was free.

"Hello, Brian." She ignored his snide congratulations. "Did you wish to see Clint?"

He cast a disinterested glance at Clint's closed door. "Yes, but there's no rush." His glance swung back to her. "Deb, I hope there's no hard feelings between us. There's no reason we can't be friends."

Being friends with Brian wasn't high on her need list, but she nodded, then added, "I'll tell Clint you came by." She reached for her message pad.

He leaned toward her. "I've missed you, darling," he murmured, his smile taking on an intimacy that disgusted her. Already he was exercising his charm on a woman other than his wife.

"Well, I didn't miss you," she came back smartly.

Instead of being insulted, he smiled his plastic smile and looked right into her eyes. "You don't mean that, you know you don't." Conceit oozed from him. "I still love you. Nothing's changed."

Disgust again washed over her. "Everything's changed. You're married, although you already seem to have forgotten that!"

"My God, Laurie's such a kid." He shrugged with blatant indifference, an indifference that made Debra feel sick inside. "I'll keep her happy enough," he said confidently, "but there's no reason you and I can't be friends." His voice had dropped, had become low and seductive. "We'd have to be careful, of course, but we can continue to see each other."

"How dare you suggest that to me!"

"Aw, Deb, don't be like that," he pleaded.

"I suggest, Brian, that you devote all your attention to your wife." Debra's voice was low and angry. "Leave me alone!"

Brian got no chance to respond, for at that moment the door to Clint's office opened.

"I'll relay your opinions on the contract to my father when he returns," Clint was saying to his visitors as he ushered them into the outer office. A scowl wiped the pleasant expression from his face when he caught sight of Brian sitting on the edge of her desk.

"We appreciate your seeing us on such short notice, Clint," one of the men replied. "Your suggestions should prove invaluable."

Debra could almost feel the effort it took for Clint to recover his equilibrium, to smile at his guests. The three men shook hands, the visitors departed, and Clint again turned to her and Brian, his stare hard on her for a moment before it shifted to Brian. She was amused to see Brian immediately stand upright.

"Are you here to see me, Brian?" Clint's tone was dry.

Brian shuffled his feet. "Of course."

His tone lacked conviction, and Clint's face went rigid with suspicion, his eyes darting once more to her. She met the recrimination in his glance with a glare of her own. Could she help it if Brian chose to be a pest?

"I've finished your report, Clint." She lifted the report and all but shoved it into his hands.

He flipped through the neatly typed pages. "You managed to get some work done, I see." The sarcasm was only thinly veiled.

"I haven't had many interruptions," she said with a bite. She clenched her hands in her lap, afraid of what she might do if she didn't.

Clint fixed her with one of his deliberate stares. "How's Laurie?" He barely glanced at Brian, though the question was obviously addressed to him. "Did the two of you enjoy Hawaii?"

Debra sighed. *Yes, I know Brian's just back from his honeymoon*, she felt like snapping. *You don't have to remind me with every breath that Brian's married to your sister.*

"Laurie's fine." Brian's heartiness was forced. "As for Hawaii, well, we were on our honeymoon."

Debra couldn't help thinking what a well-deserved jolt Brian would get when he learned his wife considered her marriage to him a mistake. Evidently he thought he could throw his association with another woman in Laurie's face and that she would forgive and forget. Debra suspected their troubles went much deeper than this easily resolved misunderstanding. Laurie must have more substantial reasons for regretting her hasty marriage.

Now Clint abruptly gestured toward his office, and Brian swaggered through ahead of him. Debra kept her face expressionless when Clint once again turned to her. She merely nodded when he asked her to place some calls for him. She was furious with him.

Moments later, when she put through the first call, she wondered if Clint might be making Brian wait on purpose. Clint had little respect for Brian, she knew that, and evidently he would only go so far in being civil to his new brother-in-law.

Well, dinner with Clint tonight was definitely out. If he thought she would sit back meekly and take this kind of treatment, he could think again. For that matter, maybe he would want to call off their date. That thought only added to her displeasure.

To think that only this morning she'd been feeling weak with the anticipation of another evening with him. She grabbed some filing, not trusting her ability to type accurately in her present mood. Just because she loved him didn't mean she'd let Clint vent his moods on her. The sooner he learned that, the better. For a moment she wished she could explain about Brian, but to do so could very easily lead to her inadvertently disclosing Laurie's confidence. She couldn't take that chance.

But her temper didn't allay the sinking sensation she felt. Why had Brian turned up at precisely the wrong moment? She and Clint had started anew this morning. She laid her forehead against the cold steel of the file cabinet. Their fresh start hadn't lasted long, that was certain, and the blame for that rested solely at Clint's feet. His accusations had not been put into words. There hadn't been the need. Clint's eyes were very eloquent. Or maybe she was beginning to understand him better.

The buzzer sounded, and when she answered it, Clint's impersonal voice asked her to place another call. Her tone in reply emulated his.

Another twenty minutes passed, and this time when the buzzer sounded, it was Clint instructing her to come in.

Clint's gaze was fixed on her as she crossed the office. Brian, she noticed, was fidgeting in his chair. Despite her distress, she felt a smile pull at her lips. Clint was keeping Brian waiting purposely; what's more, Brian knew it. Being a brother-in-law wasn't going to get him preferential treatment, Clint would see to that.

"I'd like two copies of these, please." Clint handed her a stack of legal documents.

"Certainly." Her tone was formal, and she left the office as quickly as she had entered it.

She was halfway down the hall, having first informed the switchboard operator she would be away from her desk, when she remembered she had several other copies to run. She retraced her steps.

The murmur of men's voices warned her she must have forgotten to shut Clint's door. Her own footsteps were silent over the plush carpeting. About to sort through the papers on her desk, she suddenly stopped, frozen.

"When you said you'd take Debra off my hands, Clint, I never expected you to promote her." Brian's tone insinuated all manner of things.

"Brad Johnson recommended her highly." There was a definite edge to Clint's voice, and a warning.

Brian's sly laughter made Debra grit her teeth. "Oh come on, I know you did it to get her away from me."

Debra's hands balled against her sides, and she held her breath waiting for Clint's denial.

"I did it for Laurie, not you," Clint retorted curtly.

"I know that," Brian blustered, "but from what I've heard, you've been seeing Debra away from the office." Now there was definite spite in his voice.

"When I undertake a project, I do a thorough job. Forget Debra. I'll handle her."

Handle her! Of all the…! Debra gripped the back of her chair and took several deep, steadying breaths. Shock rampaged through her in wave after humiliating wave. How could Clint talk about handling her as if she were a…a thing, not a woman! And a woman, moreover, who loved him with all of her heart!

She hugged herself around the middle. If she hadn't heard those words from his mouth, she never would have believed Clint could sound so cruel, so conniving. She had given him her love and trust, while all she had been to him was a pawn in his campaign to protect his sister.

She'd done it again; she'd allowed herself to be tricked by a man. With Brian she'd thought she'd been heartbroken; she hadn't even learned the meaning of the word. Clint's betrayal was more than she could stand. Tears would not come, the wound was too deep, though her eyes felt as if they had been rubbed with sandpaper. Her throat burned.

And then the pride that she had begun to question the merits of, rose to guide her. She straightened and, being careful not to make any sound, tiptoed from her office, the documents Clint wanted copied in her hands.

She fanned her temper, knowing it could be her salvation. It was agonizingly difficult, but she mastered her initial instincts—instincts dictated by emotion and not clear thinking. She would not run off like a heartbroken idiot, nor would she march into Clint's office and tell him what she thought of him. In the first place, she would be advertising her heartache; in the second, she would be admitting that she had overheard his conversation, which he would probably misconstrue as eavesdropping.

By the time she'd run the copies and returned to her office, she'd made her plans. She smoothed down her hair, plastered a secretarial smile on her face, knocked lightly on Clint's door and entered at his request.

Clint's smile when he thanked her for the copies sent a shaft of pain through her heart, but she didn't let on. He'd obviously recovered from his irritation with her at finding Brian draped over her desk.

She didn't say a word until she was about to leave. She paused at the door and turned to look back at him, still with the impersonal smile on her face. He stopped his discussion with Brian to send her an inquiring look.

"I have to break our date for tonight, Clint." Her tone made it clear she in no way regretted her change of plans.

"A friend has come to town, and I promised to have dinner with him."

She kept her face expressionless, even in the wake of Clint's obvious astonishment and sudden scowl. Before he could say anything, she left his office and closed the door quietly behind her.

Chapter Eight

What the hell do you mean, you're ditching me for some other man tonight?"

The sudden verbal attack made Debra jump as she was opening her car door. Clint loomed beside her, his tense body intimidating in his rage.

She avoided looking at him and tossed her shoulder bag into her car so it landed on the passenger side. "I told you, he's someone from out of town."

"Tough! Let him phone someone else. You're having dinner with me." His hand closed over her elbow.

She gave him a level look. "I've changed my mind."

"I'm not used to being stood up!"

Is that all her refusal meant to him? The high and mighty Clint Rasmussen had been stood up! Somehow she managed a nonchalant shrug. "Don't take it personally, Clint." How dare he glare down at her as if she were in the wrong; yet she couldn't stop loving him. God, she was a fool!

Clint's hand tightened on her arm. "What happened to that warm, responsive woman of this morning?"

"I don't know what you mean," she snapped, her nerves strained.

He leaned over her. "Don't give me that. You were every bit as keen for us to have dinner tonight as I was, so what's changed your mind?"

"I told you, a friend came into town." Her tone was curt.

He sucked in his breath, and when she ventured a glance at his puzzled, angry face, she could guess at the questions whizzing around in his head. This morning she had been eager to go out with him again. After the shoddy trick he had played on her, he deserved to be in the dark, to wonder what had caused her sharp reversal of mood. For that matter, his mood would hardly improve if she told him what she knew.

"Who is this friend, and what is he to you?" he demanded through set teeth.

She sighed and pretended to be bored with his questions and with him. Exasperation, contrived to hide her heartbreak, cloaked her features as she made a great play of glancing about at the employees now filing to their cars. Several people were looking at them with sharp curiosity.

"You're feeding the office gossip mill," she pointed out to him.

He hesitated, his eyes following hers. "You're right." Without releasing her, he reached around her and scooped up her handbag and flung its strap over her shoulder. "We're going to my place. You have some explaining to do."

"Oh, no I'm not!" she muttered, a blind rage at his arrogance taking hold of her. There was no way she would let him order her around. She tried to jerk free, then caught sight of two secretaries staring at them with their eyes round with disbelief. Abruptly she stopped struggling. "Let go of me!" she ordered in a low voice, intent on deflecting further attention from them.

"No!"

"You're causing a scene!"

"Too bad," Clint snapped. "You're the one who's hung up on keeping appearances."

"I should think you would be, too," she muttered furiously. "Think of your position. Do you want everyone talking about us?"

"Make no mistake, Red, you're coming with me, willing or otherwise." He brought his face close to hers, his mouth determined. "Now, are you going to walk over to my car, or do I carry you?"

"You wouldn't!"

"Try me."

He would, too. Resolve was in every line of his body. Much as it galled her, he had the upper hand, unless she wanted to broadcast their disagreement and the reasons for it to anyone nosy enough to listen.

"All right, then, let's get it over with," she retorted with poor grace.

"I thought you'd see reason."

Her only reply to that remark was a glare meant to shrivel him in his tracks, but it did nothing of the kind. If anything, it appeared to afford him a measure of satisfaction, judging by his expression.

"What about my car," she protested, holding back.

"Give me your keys. I'll see it's delivered to you later this evening." He strode toward his car, his hand firm on her elbow.

"It must be nice ordering people to do your bidding," she jeered as he released her arm and she slid into the luxury of his Continental. "Maybe your lackey has other plans for this evening."

Clint slammed the car door with unnecessary force. She'd annoyed him with her remark, and she was glad.

He threw her a sharp glance as he slid behind the wheel. "You're maligning an ambitious college kid who's only too happy to earn extra money."

Silenced, and feeling ashamed for her remark, she pulled her ignition key from her key ring and slapped it on the dash. Without a word, Clint lifted it and dropped it in his jacket pocket.

But her smoldering temper would not allow her to be silent for long. Once he'd driven from the parking lot, she rounded on him with every intention of telling him in no uncertain terms what she thought of his tactics, but he forestalled her.

"Don't, Debra." He swept a glance over her indignant face. "I can't drive and listen to you railing at me at the same time. Keep it until later."

She swallowed her retort, but the look she threw him would have quelled a lesser man. "You'll make me late for my date," she said instead.

His sharp indrawn breath was the only evidence he had caught her dig. That he was storing it in his mind for later, she didn't doubt for one minute. His controlled anger filled her with awe and fear. With deep grooves in his lean cheeks and harsh lines about his mouth, he looked older, more formidable.

The remainder of the drive was made in constrained silence. In less than twenty minutes Clint pulled to the curb in front of a huge, rambling, one-storied residence, its walls of shimmering mirrored windows designed so occupants could look out while preventing outsiders from peering in. The instant Clint cut the engine, Debra stepped from the car, preventing him from going through the gentlemanly motions of opening the door for her.

The sound of the waves crashing to shore nearby brought back painful memories of that night when Clint had asked her to go to his house with him, and she had refused. That night she might have been impressed by the immaculate grounds and sheer expanse of the house, but right now all she could think about was how she was going to dodge Clint's questions, how she was going to hide her love from him.

He came around the hood of his car and again took her arm as if he suspected she might run away. "I'd visualized your first visit here as being quite different." He looked into her eyes.

She thought it wiser to ignore that look. It would be easy to let down her defenses; love could yet defeat her. She lifted her head. At all costs she would prevent Clint from seeing behind her composed facade. He was far too perceptive.

He opened one of the carved oak double doors and waved her ahead of him into a spacious entryway, its parquet floor adorned with a wine and royal blue Persian rug. An oval gilt-framed mirror hung on the wall above a crescent-shaped rosewood table. But Clint didn't allow her to tarry, to admire, even if she had wanted to, the discriminating grandeur of his home. In any case, she was too strung up to admire anything, her nerves stretched beyond endurance. With Clint's hand on her back, she was hustled along to a mammoth sunken living room where a cream, nubby-weaved sofa, almost the width of the room, was situated in a semicircle facing the window.

Outdoors, fading sunlight glistened on the Pacific, and despite her chaotic emotions, Debra was drawn to the window.

"Your view is breathtaking," she said quite sincerely.

"I like it." He followed her and touched her arm. She didn't resist when he turned her to face him. A residue of anger remained in his eyes, but some of the tension was gone from the lines about his mouth. "I didn't bring you here to admire the view, Debra. Come and sit down."

She looked at her watch. "I haven't much time."

Glancing up at him, she caught the gathering storm in his eyes. She lifted a negligent shoulder and crossed the thick persimmon-colored carpeting to sink down on the sofa. Immediately she felt lost in the mounds of cushions that seemed to stretch on endlessly.

"Would you like a cocktail?" Clint asked. He walked to an intricately carved liquor cabinet, then glanced back at her, awaiting her reply.

She shook her head, but he returned to hand her a glass of white wine anyway. Rather than make a fuss and refuse it, she sipped the wine and found it pleasant and somewhat fortifying.

Clint removed his jacket and tossed it over the end of the sofa. The cushions depressed as he sat beside her. Loosening his tie and taking a deep swallow of some dark amber liquid in a stubby glass, he grimaced as if his drink were too strong, swishing the ice around before taking another swallow. Then he set his glass on a low marble table and turned to her.

"Do you want to phone your date and tell him you can't see him tonight?" he asked silkily.

She crossed her legs and refused to look at him. "No. If you aren't too long-winded, I'll still make it."

He lounged back. "I wouldn't count on it. I wouldn't want you to stand him up."

She set her wineglass on the table. "Look, you dragged me here against my will. So let's get this inquisition over. I don't have all night to waste."

"On me," he finished softly.

"That's right." Brave words but she was shaking inside.

"You're trying my patience, Red!" The hand resting on his knee clenched.

"That's easily resolved. Drive me back to my car and I'll be off." She gave a breezy wave.

His sun-bleached brows drew together. "The more I think of it, I believe you made up this other date for reasons I can't fathom."

She gaped at him, then quickly looked away and tried to disguise her unease. "Do you imagine you're the only man I'm dating?" She managed a light mocking laugh over the ache in her throat.

Very gently, he turned her face to his. "To be blunt, I don't believe you've been juggling dates between me and someone else. You aren't the type to two-time on a man, not when things are getting serious," he told her softly. "I had every right to be angry when you walked out of my office after announcing our date was off." He stroked the underside of her chin. "You don't fib very well. Every time I mention this other man, you avoid looking at me."

"That's not true," she protested feebly.

He leaned toward her, his lips inches from her own. "Admit it, because believe me, honey, you look the picture of guilt."

She pulled away from the temptation of those lips. "Why would I pretend to have another date if I haven't," she scoffed, hoping she sounded convincing.

His eyes bored into hers as he straightened away from her. "Perhaps you're confused. Perhaps you've discov-

ered after seeing him again that you still feel something for
Brian, or—"

"For heaven's sake." Debra scrambled to her feet and
set her hands on her hips. "You can't believe that, not after—"

"After what, Debra?" Clint asked quietly, standing beside her.

She refused to answer. Instead she tilted her chin and
made herself meet his gaze. Those blue eyes staring into
hers weakened her intent, but pride came to her aid.

"So what if I don't have another date tonight?" she
admitted with a lift of one shoulder. She didn't like white
lies and hadn't, it appeared, the expertise to carry them off.
"Frankly, Clint, I just don't want to go out with you."

For a few seconds the silence was total. A dull red seeped
beneath Clint's tan, and his body went rigid. She thought
she glimpsed hurt in his eyes as well as anger, but she must
have been mistaken, for it was temper, hot and uncon-
trolled, that blazed from his gaze as his hands gripped her
upper arms.

"You run hot and cold, don't you?"

She tried to wiggle free without success. "Not normally." She threw back her head. "Your case is an exception."

"I know a sure way of melting your ice." His mouth a
straight line, he drew her hard against him.

Despite everything, she felt something stir within her at
the contact of his muscled chest against the softness of her
breasts, an electric charge that went right through her thin
suit and blouse. "You wouldn't use sex to win your own
way, would you?" she taunted.

"Why not?" he stunned her by retorting. His mouth
softened, and he nuzzled the side of her neck, sending little shivers through her. "But we haven't progressed that

far," he murmured against her skin, "so how can you accuse me of using sex." He raised his head and looked deeply into her eyes. "Making love is what I think of when I think of you, not sex just for the sake of personal gratification." A tiny smile lifted the corners of his lips. "Right now, I'd settle for a kiss, one freely given."

"No!" She pushed violently against his shoulders, as the moment in her office when all her dreams had come to an abrupt end returned with sickening clarity.

Taken by surprise, Clint allowed her to step away. He looked pale beneath his tan.

"Okay, out with it," he demanded harshly. "Why this sudden aversion to me?"

"I owe you no explanations." Her voice cracked.

His eyes narrowed. "Something has happened to make you act this way." His gaze ran over her as if she would give him some clue unconsciously. He reached down for his drink and took a deep swallow, his eyes never leaving her, and suddenly there was realization in his gaze. He put down his glass.

"Ah, so that's it. Have you been indulging in a little eavesdropping, Debra?"

"I don't know what you mean."

"Come on, now, be truthful."

She resented the bantering note in his voice that made light of a conversation that had disillusioned her so completely.

"I did not eavesdrop!" she exploded, glad finally that everything was out in the open. "Your door was ajar."

"And who left it ajar, may I ask?"

"I didn't do it purposely." Her green eyes sparked with righteous anger and a hurt she couldn't disguise.

"Deb..." He reached for her, remorse on his face.

She evaded him. "Now, will you drive me to my car or home? I have nothing more to say to you."

He shoved his hands in his hip pockets and sighed. "It's not what you think. You should know better than to believe Brian."

"It's not Brian's words that stick in my mind," she retorted, "but yours. How dare you say you'll handle me." She choked up for several moments before she could continue. "Our whole relationship has been built on a lie, on your scheme to come between Brian and me."

He paled. "That's not true. You can't believe that!" He raked his fingers through his hair.

She walked over and lifted her shoulder bag from the sofa. "I'd like to leave now," she told him with stilted politeness.

He made no move toward the door. "Do you really mean it? Can you really walk away—" he snapped his fingers "—just like that, without trying to reach some kind of understanding?"

"Understanding! What do you take me for, a complete and utter fool?" She gave a tiny, bitter laugh. "I know what I heard, Clint. I don't need to be hit over the head to know why you've been so attentive. It's a pity you couldn't believe that Laurie and Brian had nothing to fear from me. You would have saved yourself a lot of wasted effort."

He muttered an expletive. "It's you and I that I'm concerned about, not Laurie, much as I care what happens to her."

"How very admirable." She started across the room.

He stalked after her. "Damn it, Debra, I've been seeing you because I want to, and that's the truth."

"Don't add to your lies," she said over her shoulder, the hardness in her tone belying her misery. "I won't fall for the same line twice. You're as conniving as Brian, and I, it now appears, didn't learn a thing the first time around.''

He caught her arm and turned her towards him, his arms around her back forcing her to brace herself against his chest. "You can't go, Deb, not like this." His voice was hoarse with emotion.

She pushed against his chest. "Let me go, Clint." She was suddenly exhausted with arguing and fighting the inclination to throw herself into his arms no matter how much he had deceived her. That she could feel this way after what he had done made her question her sanity.

But instead of releasing her, he pressed his cheek to hers. For a split second her love for him took control, and she closed her eyes in the exquisite pain of wanting to stay there cradled in his arms, even if the pressure of his cheek on hers seemed more a gesture of affection rather than passion or love. But as much as she longed for it all—affection, passion, love—she had no use for an affection spawned by guilt. Perhaps he did regret hurting her, for he must know she was hurting inside. Perhaps she hadn't mistaken his nature completely. Perhaps some inherent decency made him have regrets, now that she'd faced him with her knowledge of his deception.

His pity was the last thing she wanted. She met the intentness of his gaze with a frigid stare. "I'm a woman, not a child, Clint. I don't need to be patted and coddled. You may have played me for a fool, but I assure you, I'll bounce back readily enough."

One of his hands slid up her back and he started to knead the taut muscles of her neck. "I'm sure you will, but what you're thinking is all wrong, Deb. I admit I told Brian I'd take you off his hands." He tightened his hold when she would have broken from his grasp. "But I forgot all about that once I got to know you."

"How convenient. And I daresay you'll forget this conversation, too, when it suits you."

He gave her a slight shake. "Such harsh words from lips meant for kissing, not sarcasm. I can understand why you feel as you do, but how can I convince you otherwise if you're too stubborn to listen?"

"Quite a dilemma, isn't it? You'll just have to accept defeat. You can't win every time."

"Accept defeat? Oh no, not where you're concerned. There's too much at stake." And with that his lips came down on hers, coaxing and seductive.

She knew she should resist him. No matter what he said, he had deceived her. Common sense, if not pride, dictated that she should push him away, but all she could think of was that this would be the last time he would ever hold her. When she walked out the door, there would be no turning back. It would be over.

The pain at that thought was intense, and she moaned against his lips, her own mouth parting at his soft, probing insistence. She clutched at his broad shoulders, her heart starting to hammer as his hands slid beneath her short jacket.

He touched her breast, then lifted his head a fraction. "You're heart's pounding, love," he whispered huskily. He brought one of her hands down so he could press it against his chest. "And see, my heart's pounding too. How can you deny what we do to each other?"

He didn't wait for her answer. His lips again seared hers, and the heat of his body scorched through her clothing until she was aware of every part of him, aware of the desire that surged within him. She whimpered a halfhearted protest when he swept her up in his arms and carried her to the sofa, but his caresses dulled her objection, faint though it was, and she reclined across his lap. Instead her lips welcomed his again, and she sighed at the fiery possession as she stroked the smoothness of his shirtfront, then opened the buttons so she could caress his warm skin.

Clint groaned and, with hands that trembled, he removed her jacket and started unbuttoning her blouse. "No, you mustn't," she murmured, yet made no move to stop him when he unerringly found her bra snap and released it. His palm caressed her breasts, his thumb rubbing over one nipple, causing spasms of pleasure to shoot through her until she was instinctively arched against him, a soft cry breaking from her when his lips claimed the rosy tip.

"You're exquisite," he muttered from deep in his throat, lifting his head for an instant to afford her other breast the same attention, the sensation making her shake in his arms. "I want you, sweetheart." His eyes searched hers confidently, expecting agreement, as if they hadn't been arguing moments before.

I want you. The words drummed through her head like so many tiny hammers and jolted her upright. She scrambled from his lap, and Clint, taken unawares, made no attempt to restrain her.

What was she doing letting him caress her so intimately? She was mad, utterly mad! She burned with shame. She loved him, but he was using her to...to satisfy his...his ego, and what was worse, his male need.

Difficult though it was, she had her blouse buttoned before he rose beside her. "Well, I don't want you," she lied vehemently as she lifted her shoulder bag that had fallen on the floor.

He calmly buttoned his shirt. "Liar," was all he said, but that one word said it all.

Since no clever answer occurred to her, she remained silent. Hands still unsteady, she tried to tidy her hair, which had come tumbling down during their session on the sofa, then gave up the task with a shaken sigh. She started for the door, then hesitated. She should phone for a taxi; they didn't cruise in residential areas. In the circumstances, she didn't want Clint driving her. She hadn't broken down yet, but wasn't sure how long she could keep up this pretense. Just then Clint came up beside her. He had his jacket on and obviously still intended to drive her home.

He stepped in front of her, facing her, and startled, she glanced up to see him staring down at her, a nerve throbbing in his temple.

"Let's quit this cat-and-mouse game, Debra. Marry me."

Utterly flabbergasted, she stared up at him. "You're out of your mind!" she exclaimed, a catch in her voice, her heartbeat drumming in her ears.

"Am I? Deny it all you like, but you want me as much as I want you," he accused gruffly.

"Want! Is that all you men think about?" she cried.

"At least I'm offering marriage, which is more than that poor excuse for a man, Brian, ever did!" He laughed harshly. "Pardon me, now I remember, he did mention marriage, didn't he?

"You bas—" Her voice shook with temper and hurt. "I should never have confided in you, never given you the chance to throw that back in my face."

"Hell, Deb," he cupped her face in his hands, "you have me so mixed up, blowing hot one minute and sub-zero the next, I don't know what I'm saying half the time."

It was quite an admission from a man as self-assured as Clint, and for a moment she weakened, even swayed toward him. Then she straightened and moved out of reach.

"You're right, Clint." She sounded as weary as she felt. "You don't know what you're saying."

"Yes I do. Say yes, sweetheart, and we'll drive to Vegas tonight."

Her heart leaped, but no words of love followed his impassioned declaration. A terrible coldness crept through her. He wasn't even pretending to love her; yet he talked of marriage. And once he possessed her—for he apparently thought she had been holding out for marriage and for no other reason—he could, conceivably, be just as casual when he suggested divorce.

"No, I will not marry you!" She yanked open the door.

"Not so fast." A hard grip on her arm detained her. "I won't ask you a second time, Debra," he warned, looking down at her coldly, "but if you change your mind, let me know."

Chapter Nine

That night, lying in bed, Debra wondered how she'd managed to refuse Clint's proposal, when she loved him with all of her being. Did it matter if his desire for her was temporary? If she had accepted, would the love she felt for him, in time, have been returned?

Once again she pulled the blanket over her shoulders. She had turned over but still couldn't get comfortable. No matter how she tried to block out the memory of Clint's passionate kisses and the touch of his hands, her mind had a will of its own and paid no heed to her silent entreaty. She could still feel the warmth of his lips on her breasts, as if he were beside her in her narrow single bed.

The drive home had been fraught with tension. Clint had stared straight ahead, and she'd found no way to bridge the gulf between them. He didn't look at her until they arrived at her town house. When he leaned across her to open the door, her instinctive shrinking against the upholstery lest he touch her made him give her an utterly scathing look. That look, more than words, told her how he viewed her belated reticence.

Even now, hours later, his parting words filled her with a feeling of doom, of an impasse that only she could scale.

"You have no monopoly on pride, Debra. I have my share."

Now his words seemed to reverberate off the walls of her bedroom. With a soft cry she pressed her hands to her ears and buried her face in her pillow. If only she could sleep.

Weariness proved her ally, and sleep eventually claimed her, though she awoke more than once that night. When her alarm rang next morning, she felt she hadn't slept at all. Her first thought was that none of it had happened. It was too bizarre, Clint asking her to marry him after knowing her such a short time, and never once saying he loved her. Her second thought was that she couldn't face him this morning, or any time soon, not while her emotions were in such turmoil.

Still, she got up and showered; but instead of dressing as she normally would, she went down to the kitchen in her robe.

Her mother frowned as she walked in. "Dear, you don't look at all well, and you hardly ate anything for dinner last night."

She hadn't told her mother about Clint's proposal; she'd been too torn apart inside to talk about it. Although she now felt more composed, she still couldn't talk about it. How could you explain to your mother that you felt a man desired you, but did not necessarily love you, a proposal of marriage notwithstanding?

"I have a pounding headache," Debra admitted. And no wonder. She'd spent a good part of the night fighting tears, until her eyes felt gritty.

"Stay home, then. I'm sure Clint will understand."

Her mother's suggestion provided an easy way out, and for a moment, Debra considered doing as she suggested. Then she shook her head, the very motion making her head ache all the more.

"No, I have to go in, Mom."

Except for a concerned look, her mother didn't press her. There was no doubt she would be wondering what was going on between her and Clint, though, what with Clint dropping her off last evening and her car being delivered hours later.

To her relief, Clint's door was closed, and the telephone light indicated he was on the phone when she arrived at the office an hour later. She felt sick in the pit of her stomach and needed a few minutes to gain a semblance of self-control. She may have rejected him, ultimately, the past evening, but love had dictated her physical response to his lovemaking. All she could hope was that Clint believed desire had ruled her actions. She had shown just how much she needed him, and they both knew it. Whatever he may be, Clint was no fool.

The instant she sat behind her desk, she knew she could never carry it off. She couldn't pretend nothing had happened. Pride had made her keep on after Brian's betrayal, but Clint was a different matter. She couldn't hide her love from him indefinitely. Day after day in such close proximity, she was bound to give herself away. She had to leave, and what's more, she had to leave today.

But how could she quit without giving two weeks' notice? To just walk out could ruin her career by making a good reference impossible. Yet to give proper notice would defeat her purpose, since Clint himself would be leaving around that time. She pressed her fingertips to her temples. He would return from time to time, that was certain, and she couldn't stand the constant reminder that she could have been his wife.

Numbed, she typed her resignation, and the instant the light went out on the telephone, she tapped on his door and walked in, crossing the room to stand in front of his desk. Never had his office seemed so large, those few feet from door to desk, endless. It didn't help that the whole time Clint watched her, his eyes were cold and enigmatic.

"So, you turned up after all," he said.

She set the crisp white sheet of paper before him. "Of course." She made it sound as though the idea of staying home had never occurred to her.

"Of course," he repeated with an ironic twist of his lips, but his eyes left her face to read the short, terse resignation before he lifted his head again. "Sit down, please." His tone was formal, employer to employee, and Debra sat. In truth, now that she was facing him, she needed the support of a chair beneath her. With a look of disgust, he pitched her resignation into his pending file tray. "Running away, Debra?"

She raised her chin. "I don't see it that way." She wouldn't indulge in a heated pro and con discussion of her decision. "I've given two weeks' notice, as required, but I'd appreciate it if I could leave today."

"Would you now? That might prove inconvenient. Why say two weeks if you don't intend to stay that long?"

She sighed impatiently. "I have to if I want a good reference from the company."

"Aah!"

"Don't sound so smug! Don't you think I'd like to give in to my inclinations, to just walk out!" She glared at him. "Unlike you, I'm not wealthy. I can't afford to destroy four years of hard work by giving in to a mood."

"My ever cautious Debra."

She took a deep breath. "I don't care what you think," she lied. "If it was only myself involved, I wouldn't have come in today, but I have my mother to consider."

"So what you're asking is for me to do you a favor, to pretend your leaving in no way inconveniences me, to even, perhaps, put in a good word for you with personnel."

She threw him a look. "You don't have to go that far. Just don't make a fuss because I want to go today. I'll speak to Mr. Johnson and say I'm leaving for personal reasons. If you don't object, he certainly won't. He may even think I'm finally quitting because of Brian and be relieved." She made a face at that thought, then leaned forward to say earnestly, "You can't want me here, Clint, any more than I want to be here, not after last night."

"On the contrary, I like having you around. Why else would I have asked you to marry me?"

He might have been discussing the weather. She almost blurted out she knew darn well why he'd proposed. He wanted her in his bed and figured that marriage was her price. She bit back the words. She couldn't get on that subject, not without leading them into treacherous waters. Besides, he was waiting for her to lose her temper, a faintly mocking smile on his face as he sat there, leaning back in his chair, his hands now clasped behind his neck.

"Clint—"

His smile broadened. "Yes, dear?"

"Don't 'Yes, dear,' me like a . . . a . . ."

"Like a dutiful husband? Is that what you were going to say? Why, honey, I'm just practicing."

"Well, don't practice on me. I won't be your wife."

It cut into her to voice that truth, but she was gratified to see her retort wipe the grin from his face. His chair protested as his feet slammed to the floor and he slapped his palms on his desk.

"No? You may yet choke on those words, Red."

"Never!"

He got abruptly to his feet and strode around his desk to stare down at her, so close that he left her little room to rise as well, not without bringing herself too near to him for her peace of mind. She stared back at him and kept her expression as indifferent as she could.

"Sometimes, Deb, you tempt me to give you a good hard shake. You're so damn stubborn!"

"Me, stubborn? I just hold my own, that's all. Trouble is, you expect everyone to jump through hoops when you tell them to, and can't stand it when someone doesn't obey."

"Quite a little speech, Deb, but you're avoiding the issue. Your job is incidental."

"Not to me it isn't!"

He tipped his head to the side, looking at her beneath hooded lids. "Solve our personal problem, and all other problems will disappear."

"We don't have a personal anything." This time she did get up and stepped around him before he could stop her. "What's it to be, Clint? Do I leave today with the promise of a reference, or do I quit without it?"

"So, now you're determined to leave today no matter what the consequences. What's the matter, getting desperate?"

"No!" She threw her hands in the air. "I can't stand this bickering anymore, that's all." She marched toward the door.

"Strange," Clint mused a few steps behind her, "how you can't bear to work here with me, yet you could force yourself to stay when Brian got married."

She swung round to glower up at him. "I've learned by my mistakes. Smart people do, you know."

"Is that it, Deb? I don't think so." He took her arm and walked to the door with her, where he turned her to face him before releasing her. "The only time I get any honesty from you is when you're in my arms." He showed his teeth in a tight-lipped grimace. "Don't step back like that as if you expect me to pounce. I'm not going to touch you. Any decision you make about us is going to be with your head. I won't give you the chance to say I tricked you. You've thrown that at me too many times already."

"I've made my decision." To her chagrin, her voice shook.

The corners of his mouth lifted ever so slightly. "Don't you ever change your mind? You came in here prepared to put up with me for two weeks if you had to, but now you're leaving today without any promise from me about a reference. So you see, you can change your mind."

She pulled open the door and stalked over to her desk to lift her handbag from her drawer. Then she made herself look at him, loving everything about him, from his cropped blond hair to his intent blue eyes and firm chin. She tried not to linger on the lips that had so often driven her mindlessly toward passion. Never again would she feel herself drawn to that broad masculine chest.

For a split second she wavered, then stiffened. Marriage for her meant a lifetime commitment. Nothing Clint had said or done indicated he felt the same way. Such commitment was vital; she couldn't settle for less. Nor could she ask him to mouth words he couldn't say of his own volition.

"Anyone can change his or her mind," she told him quietly, "but not about fundamentals, not if one has any standards."

"What the hell is that supposed to mean?"

She couldn't explain, not without revealing the depth of her love. "When . . . when are you actually leaving?" The question popped out without any forethought on her part.

Clint was very still. "The date's not fixed—could be two weeks, more or less." His eyes never left her face.

She bent her head for an instant, then walked, head held high, toward the corridor, her steps hesitating only a fraction when she heard Clint speak behind her.

"I meant what I said last night, Deb."

It was a concession on his part, this oblique reference to his proposal. He wasn't asking her a second time, but he was coming as close to that as he could and still keep to his warning. She couldn't allow herself to turn around. To do so would test her determination to follow the path she had chosen. Right now she feared she might weaken, so she kept on walking, knowing he wasn't following her, that he never would again.

The next few days proved agonizing. Sometimes she couldn't believe that she had walked away from Clint.

As for the financial ramifications of leaving her job, these became more and more of a worry as she sought a similar position. Clint was right, the salary he had paid her was fantastic. She found prospective employers impressed with her qualifications, but reluctant to hire her when they could not pay her a salary comparable to what she had earned. More than one person told her she would soon become dissatisfied and leave.

She wondered if the position Clint had mentioned to her when he had wanted her to quit her job might still be available, but she certainly wouldn't ask him. She wanted no more favors. She wished she hadn't been compelled to ask his cooperation about her reference, but she had to be practical.

It bothered her that she never did get to speak to Mr. Johnson in person. She felt she owed him that courtesy, but he had been out of the office on her final day with the company. She'd phoned him the next morning, and before she could say anything, he'd informed her that Clint had explained the situation, that she need not concern herself, that he would recommend her highly to any prospective employer. She was left wondering what Clint had given as a reason for her precipitous departure, although she was grateful her impulsive action wouldn't tarnish her reputation as a reliable employee. She supposed she should phone and thank Clint, but it hurt too much to think of speaking to him again with no future together ahead of them.

But think of him she did. In truth, he was never out of her mind. Sometimes she worried whether she was applying herself enough to her job hunting, or whether her mind was too consumed with thoughts of Clint to do justice to anything else. Tomorrow would be Friday and she hadn't even a prospect in the offing.

Sighing, she glanced across the living room at her mother, who was thumbing through a magazine. Naturally she'd had to explain to her mother why she'd quit her job, had told her Clint had proposed in such an offhand way she felt he was in no way committing himself to a lifetime marriage. She hadn't touched on what she believed, that Clint merely desired her but did not love her. The humiliation of such a thought was difficult enough to accept herself, while the intimacies that had fostered that belief were between her and Clint, and no one else.

Not knowing the full story, her mother had been dismayed and told her she had been hasty. Debra smiled fondly. Her mother had been more upset about her refusing Clint than about her loss of a well-paying position.

Her mother must have felt her watching her, for she glanced up and laid aside her magazine.

"Do you want to talk about what's bothering you, dear?" Marilyn asked.

"I don't know that talking will help, Mom. I didn't expect to get another job right away, but it's more difficult than I thought." Debra tried to smile, to alleviate her mother's obvious concern. "Clint said secretaries could always get a job, but executive secretarial positions are not that easy to find. I never thought earning an excellent salary could prove a hindrance." She looked down at her hands. "You shouldn't worry, though. I have enough saved to meet my share of the bills for three months at least. I'll have a job long before then, I'm sure."

"Hush, dear! As if I care about that. It's your emotional well-being I'm worried about, and I'm well aware that it's this misunderstanding with Clint that has you looking miserable."

"Do I look that bad?" Debra tried to joke. "Besides, Clint and I had no misunderstanding. He proposed, I turned him down, and that's the end of it. Both of us know exactly where we stand."

"Why you turned him down is what I can't comprehend," Marilyn grumbled. "I know you love him. And he must love you, or why would he propose?"

"Love has nothing to do with it, Mom," Debra observed bitterly. "Anyway, who knows what Clint is thinking? He keeps his deepest feelings hidden, except..." She felt her cheeks grow hot.

"Humph! He doesn't need to get married if all he wants is a willing female, young lady. There are plenty of those about, especially for a man like Clint." Marilyn shook her head. "I'm positive you're misjudging him."

"I don't think so, Mom." Debra was beginning to feel put out that her mother could find excuses for Clint even though she had told her about his conversation with Brian. "Anyway, Mom, Clint misjudged me, didn't he, in the beginning?"

"Surely you aren't holding that against him?"

Debra's brow creased. "No, I'm not." Again she sighed. "I just don't understand him and what motivates him."

"Then ask him what he means. Choosing a lifetime partner is the most important decision you'll ever make." Marilyn waved her arms in exasperation. "Don't let stupid pride stand in your way. It isn't worth it, Debra!"

Debra got to her feet. "I've made my decision."

She'd said the same thing to Clint, but with more conviction. The three days since she'd seen him seemed more like three years. How was she going to get through the rest of her life without him?

"You can't deny you're feeling wretched!" Marilyn exclaimed.

Debra dropped a kiss on her mother's temple. "Don't get uptight about me and my problems. I know you want what is best for me, Mom, but I have to follow my own instincts."

"Instincts aren't dictating your actions," Marilyn said with certainty. "Otherwise, I'd be planning a summer wedding."

Debra gave her mother a wan smile. She couldn't deny what her mother said, but she didn't want to talk about Clint anymore. It was bad enough she would spend the night dreaming about him, or worse still, lie awake for hours thinking about him.

"How about some tea, Mom?" she asked, changing the subject as she walked toward the kitchen.

"All right, dear." Her mother's voice was resigned.

Debra had the teacups and a plate of shortbread on the tray when the doorbell rang. Moments later she could hear the murmur of voices, the sound of a deep baritone making her suddenly go weak at the knees.

Clint! What was he doing here?

"Debra," Marilyn called, and Debra heard her mother hurry along the short hallway toward the kitchen. "Clint's come to see you, dear." The buoyant note in her mother's voice was all too apparent.

"Hello, Debra, how's the job hunting going?" Clint stopped in the doorway to the kitchen while her mother stood beside him, beaming at them both.

"Nothing so far," she replied when she could find her voice, her hungry eyes devouring him even while she wanted to denounce him for coming. He knew she'd had no intention of ever seeing him once she'd quit her job. That was the whole reason for quitting, for heaven's sake.

He looked fabulous, as always. Tonight he wore a camel hair jacket with leather patch elbows and slacks of a deep chocolate brown. His open-necked shirt, in the same rich shade of brown, outlined his hard muscular chest.

Debra was suddenly conscious she hadn't a smidgen of makeup on, and her simple cotton shirt and blouse couldn't compete with the smart casualness of Clint's attire.

But maybe loving a man made a woman see more than that which appeared on the surface, she mused. The direct way Clint's blue eyes met hers made her want to drown in their clear depths, though she recognized their challenge. Clint was warning her, without saying a word, that if she made a fuss in front of her mother about his coming, he wouldn't back down, that she would be the one who was embarrassed if there was a scene.

"Well, put another cup on the tray," her mother admonished her gaily, breaking the awkward silence.

Debra welcomed the chance to turn away to get another cup. She could feel Clint's gaze on the back of her neck while she poured boiling water into the teapot, and when the tray was ready, he lifted it before she could.

"You lead the way, ladies," he said with a grin, and they all trooped the short distance to the living room, with Debra feeling more nervous every second.

Her mother automatically took over the tea pouring so Debra didn't have that ceremony to hide behind. Instead, when she looked across the room at Clint seated opposite, her gaze again locked with his. He looked relaxed, lazing back in his chair, and she suddenly felt resentful that he appeared nowhere near as disturbed as she was.

"I didn't expect you to drop in," she said to Clint after first sipping some tea. Her tone made it plain she neither expected nor wanted his visit.

Her mother made a faint disapproving sound beside her, but Clint merely lifted one brow and gave her a wry look.

"I thought if you were having any problem finding a job, you might want to contact that firm I told you about some time ago."

"I'll manage on my own," she said with a touch of asperity.

Clint turned to her mother and smiled affably. "Has she been this grumpy all week?"

Marilyn chuckled. "Don't tease her, Clint."

Debra glared at both of them. "Being unemployed is hardly a teasing matter."

"You chose to quit," Clint reminded her, voice dry.

Her mother patted her on the arm. "Now, dear, don't get upset."

"I'm not," Debra said with a faint smile for her mother's benefit, but it disappeared the instant she looked at Clint. "I had valid reasons for quitting, as you know perfectly well."

"Shall we delve into those reasons?" Clint's glance flicked to her mother then back to Debra.

Her mother set her cup on the cocktail table. "I'll run upstairs and leave you two to have this discussion in private."

"No, Mom," Debra exclaimed, and glared at Clint at the same time.

"No need for you to run off," Clint seconded Debra's protest. "There's nothing I'll say that you can't hear, Marilyn." The glance he directed at Debra cautioned her that the tone of any discussion was her responsibility.

Her mother looked from one to the other of them, then got to her feet and gestured for Clint to remain seated as he, too, rose. "I have a favorite television show to watch, and I'll watch it on the small set in my room."

"You needn't leave on my account," Clint reiterated, looking uncomfortable, yet determined.

This time it was Clint's arm her mother patted. "You two settle your differences," Marilyn chided gently.

To Debra's surprise, Clint leaned down and kissed her mother on her cheek, much as she had done just minutes before he arrived. "We'll try," he promised, and didn't resume his seat until her mother had disappeared up the stairs.

"Now look what you've done, you've driven my mother from her own living room." Debra knew she was being unfair, but at the moment she didn't much care.

His tea untouched, Clint sat back in his chair, his arms across his chest. "I did no such thing. It's your belligerence that made your mother feel in the way,'' he pointed out bluntly.

"I am not belligerent!"

"Oh, yes you are. You've been dying to fight with me from the minute I arrived. All I've done is show a friendly interest in your career." He looked almost pious.

"I know first-hand what your interest in my career entails!"

"Sarcastic again? You've developed some unattractive qualities lately, Debra."

She held on to her temper. "I'm suitably grateful for your friendly overture," she said with the same brand of sarcasm, "but I'll find my own job, thank you."

His jaw clenched. "It's a shame your father wasn't around when you were growing up to teach you some manners."

"My father would never have spanked me," she rebuked sharply. "Anyway, Dad had only to frown at me," she added, voice soft, "and I was in tears and promising to be good."

The flash of temper in Clint's eyes faded. "Poor little kid," he murmured. "You worshiped him, didn't you?"

She thought a moment. "I guess so. He was my father and I loved and respected him."

"Don't you think it's time for you to love and respect another man, time for you to find a husband?"

"I'm in no hurry. The modern woman has other options in case you didn't know."

"A man has always had options," he countered with a touch of whimsy, "but even the most confirmed bachelor eventually chooses a wife."

"Why does a 'confirmed bachelor' decide to marry?" she asked. "As you say, he does have other options." Despite the pertness of her remark, she trembled and held her breath for his answer.

But Clint took his time before speaking. He seemed to be mulling over his reply. "A man tires of casual affairs, Debra. That's okay for a while—even preferable, from a man's viewpoint—but there comes a time when a home and family become important. And that, confirmed bachelor or not, usually means he has to marry."

"Reluctantly, no doubt," Debra said tartly. Love, it seemed, figured nowhere in Clint's calculations.

"Perhaps."

Clint's tone was aloof and noncommittal, giving her no idea as to his own feelings. That rankled—and hurt. She got to her feet and hoped he'd get the message.

Clint also rose, but he made no motion to leave. "Would you like to go to dinner tomorrow?" he asked.

She gave him a startled—and dismissive—look. "I'm surprised you'd ask," she exclaimed. "I made it plain when I quit that I never, ever, wanted to see you again."

He looked down at her from his superior height. "I know why you quit, but that was your decision. It has nothing to do with my intentions or actions."

And with that, he drew her into his arms.

Chapter Ten

Debra's eyelashes fluttered downward, and unable to stop herself, she lifted her face, every part of her in a haze of wanting. Her hunger for him made her grab greedily at this last chance to feel his lips on hers. What harm could a few stolen moments in his arms do? She was conscious of his hands on her back, the muscular hardness of his wide shoulders beneath her palms, unaware until then that she had instinctively raised her hands to rest them there, not to push him away, but to glory in the broadness of his chest, his strength. Contrasted with that superb masculine body, her own seemed softer, more feminine, more sensual.

But the kiss she waited for didn't come, and her eyes flew open to meet Clint's bland expression.

"For a woman who doesn't want to see me, you certainly do pucker up at the least provocation," he drawled.

Her face flamed, and she wrenched free. In that instant she hated him every bit as much as she loved him.

"You swine!"

He shrugged, though his eyes looked like ice-blue slivers in a face rigid with anger. "I'll let you get away with that this time, but don't think I'll always be so easy." He cupped her face in his hands. "Promise me you'll think about us," he said. The cold eyes warmed a fraction, became intense, as if by sheer force of will he would convince her to his way of thinking.

"I—I have." She despised herself for that break in her voice, especially seconds after he had trapped her into revealing, once again, how willing she was to go into his arms.

Fair brows met across the bridge of his nose. "No you haven't, you've reacted. You've climbed back inside that armor of yours." He sighed wearily. "It's unfortunate you had to overhear that particular conversation."

"Unfortunate!" Her voice was shrill, and she stared at him.

He swore under his breath. "Forget what you overheard, Debra. It means nothing. Think about your future, and mine."

"We don't have a future," she muttered, aching inside.

"We could have." His hands dropped to his sides.

She wondered how a man so knowledgeable about women could believe she could dismiss what she had overheard as if it were of no consequence. Even if she could, she would never forget it. Those seconds were carved into her brain. After her earlier qualms, when Clint frankly admitted he saw her as a threat to his sister's marriage, she'd thought that she had finally rid him of such misconceptions. While she had allowed her trust in him to grow, he had retained his initial distrust, except for an occasional lapse or two.

His desire for her was a complication he obviously hadn't considered; and it was that desire, as yet unsatisfied, that was driving him now. She trembled. Such lust was an insult. The superficiality of it filled her with pain.

She schooled her features into a proud, cold mask. "Clint, please go."

His face stiffened at that polite but clear dismissal. Again she witnessed the hot anger in his eyes, and she could actually feel the self-control it took for him not to shake her as he'd threatened to do. Instead he shoved his hands in his pockets.

"You're being unreasonable." His voice was harsh, his face remote. "Once you think someone has infringed on your pride, you can't see anything else."

"You don't like proud women, do you, Clint?" she taunted him. "You'd prefer it if I was a simpering little fool who would let you trample all over me, then come back and beg for more."

"Don't talk rot! But you're a little fool if you believe nothing is more important than pride. There are more important things in life."

"I know that." She was exhausted suddenly, the zest to fight him was gone.

"Do you? I wonder." He turned to open the front door. "I leave at the end of next week. I'll be gone for at least six months." He looked back at her. "A lot can happen in six months."

Meaning he could find another woman, one probably more amenable. Debra felt sick at the thought. Already he was insinuating his desire was transitory, that in six months he would, in all likelihood, change his mind. How much could his proposal mean to him, if he could think that within days of asking her to marry him? She'd been right to refuse his proposal; and if he believed pride and pride alone had motivated her, so much the better. That was certainly preferable to his knowing the truth.

She pressed her cold hands together. "Goodbye, Clint."

He made no reply, just stood there looking down at her, his expression impossible to read. In the next instant he turned from her and left.

Afterward, the tears that had been threatening for days became a flood. In a way, it was a welcome relief to give in to the heartache ripping her apart. Blindly she stumbled to the sofa and huddled there while she gave vent to a misery that would no longer be denied. Her slender body shook with the force of her weeping until she felt limp.

Tears accomplished nothing, she thought, mopping her face with some tissue. She loved Clint, but she couldn't marry him. And if she couldn't have him, she didn't want anyone else. No matter that she'd always wanted a good marriage and a career, it appeared she was destined to be a career woman and nothing more. Such single-mindedness would probably result in greater success; but when she thought of the life ahead of her without Clint's love, it appeared empty and devoid of all emotion.

In the mood or not, she still had to find another job. That necessity kept her functioning. She may have given in to her despair and heartache that one time, but it was a luxury she could not afford to repeat.

Her quest was no more successful on Friday than it had been earlier in the week. Despite her unhappiness, she made herself scrutinize the employment columns in *The Register* that weekend, and on Monday morning she contacted an employment agency. The woman interviewer assured her that with her qualifications they must be selective, but felt certain they could find a suitable position for her.

The thought that Clint was leaving at the end of the week never left her. Over and over again she tried to convince herself she was doing the right thing, but nothing could stop her yearning.

It didn't help that her mother still felt she was being foolish. All through dinner her mother had been very quiet, troubled because Debra was so miserable. It had been like that between them ever since she was a child. If one of them was disturbed about something, the other one was just as disturbed.

The comedy on television, instead of lifting Debra's mood, only succeeded in becoming an irritation. Her mother must have felt the same way, for she switched the controls to mute, then turned to her.

"Why don't you phone Clint?" Marilyn asked.

The automatic rejection that would have burst from Debra a few days ago was not forthcoming. Instead she wrung her hands and muttered, "How can I, Mom? He doesn't love me."

Her mother switched off the television altogether. "You can't be sure of that."

Debra didn't get the chance to reply, for the phone rang. She was glad of the interruption. Part of her wanted to air her troubles, while part of her wanted to ignore they existed.

A brief smile brightened her wan face when she heard Sharon's voice on the other end of the line. At first Sharon ran on about her plans for the nursery, but soon she got down to the real purpose of her call.

Gossip was rife since Debra had quit, but most people at the office thought she had left because of Brian's return. Well, that was fine with Debra; and considering the lengths she had gone to a few short weeks ago to avert such talk, it was amazing how little it mattered now. As for

Clint, it took all her willpower not to ask Sharon for news of him. Her friend obviously sensed her interest, for she supplied the information without her asking.

"They have a temporary secretary working for Clint," Sharon said. "I've heard Mr. Johnson is waiting for the senior Mr. Rasmussen's return before hiring anyone."

"That's probably best," Debra commented. "Clint's leaving, anyway, at the end of the week."

"Oh, I didn't know. You've seen him, then?"

"Yes." Debra didn't go into details, though she could hear the curiosity in Sharon's voice. Much as she valued Sharon's friendship, she'd never divulged the depth of her feeling for Clint. This wasn't because she'd wanted to protect herself from possible humiliation such as had occurred with Brian. No, it was because she feared she might become maudlin should she speak of her futile love for Clint. Now, as things had turned out, she was glad she had been discreet.

The next day, when out again on a job interview, she was vexed when she found herself driving along Clint's street and peering at his house like a teenager haunting the home of the high school's latest heartthrob.

"You need your head examined, Debra McLeod," she muttered as she roared down the street in an effort to put as much distance between her and Clint's home.

His home for the next few days, that is. With that thought, a wave of anguish washed over her.

At dinner her mother tactfully refrained from asking how her job hunting had gone that day, nor did she mention Clint. No wonder there were these long silences between them, Debra thought, as they settled in the living room afterward. She flipped through the TV Guide.

"I wish you hadn't turned Clint down quite so definitely," Marilyn said, and set aside her needlepoint. "I haven't been able to think of anything else all day."

"I know." Debra tossed the magazine on the cocktail table. "He's on both of our minds."

"If only I could help. But I can't. You have to make your own decisions."

Debra nodded and sighed, loving her mother for her concern and her truthfulness. She could tell herself time and time again that she had done the right thing in refusing Clint, but her love for him grew stronger with each passing day. Even the suspicion that he'd plotted to come between her and Brian, although unnecessary, no longer seemed as important. Instead her mind dwelled on his saying that once he knew her, he'd wanted to see her for his own sake.

Had she misjudged him?

She shook her head. She couldn't start doubting her actions. She mustn't! To consider what she had lost, if she should prove wrong, was unendurable.

Doubts persisted during the next two days. Even the prospect of an executive secretarial position could not lift her spirits. She was going through the motions of living, though she felt dead inside. But economics made her keep the appointment arranged for her by the employment agency for Thursday morning.

She dressed with care in a smoky-gray summer suit and high-heeled pumps. Once she arrived at the company in Irvine, and had completed an application form, she was ushered into the personnel manager's office.

Bald and wearing glasses, the manager, a Mr. Garcia, stood as she entered, his hand outstretched.

"Miss McLeod, I'm glad to meet you. I understand from the agency that you worked for Clint Rasmussen.

Normally I would interview someone, then check their references, but Clint's an old friend, so I gave him a call. He's out of town, but Mr. Johnson recommended you highly.''

"I'm pleased to hear that.'' She smiled in response and shook the proffered hand, wondering all the while if by luck she had applied for the very position Clint had mentioned. It was possible. Her briefing by the agency seemed to indicate so. As she well knew, there weren't that many positions of this calibre available.

Mr. Garcia indicated she should sit down and resumed his own seat. The care with which he read her application confirmed that if this was the firm Clint had spoken of, she would get the position only if she suited the company's needs and not merely because of the influence of Clint's name. If she was hired, it would be on her own merits and on the strength of Mr. Johnson's recommendation.

It was quite some time before Mr. Garcia set her application aside and looked at her. "Your experience appears to be what we want, Miss McLeod.'' He went on to mention a salary comparable to the one she had been receiving. He inquired regarding her duties at her old company and nodded his head in a satisfied way at her answers. "How soon can you start?'' he asked, smiling, when she was finished.

She tried to hide her surprise at the rapidity with which she was being hired. "Would Monday be convenient?'' she replied.

"Fine.'' He got to his feet. "You're surprised I made the offer without further consideration, aren't you?''

"Yes,'' she admitted.

"I wouldn't, normally. But if you worked for Clint Rasmussen, and he was pleased, well, that's good enough for me.''

She thought of Mr. Garcia's remark as she walked to her car. Everyone seemed to respect Clint and his opinions. Was she the only one who saw motive in everything he did? Was she wrong?

Well, she'd phone him. He deserved her thanks for seeing to it she received a good reference, and surely she was big enough to show her appreciation when it was due.

Show her appreciation? Considering their relationship, however short-lived, she could imagine Clint's reaction if she phoned and offered him her polite thank-you without referring to anything personal. He'd probably accuse her of being prim, and suggest she was using this excuse to contact him because she hadn't the courage to own up to what she really wanted to say.

And he would be right. Part of her wanted to run to him, to accept his proposal, and worry about the consequences later.

Once on the freeway, she concentrated on the traffic, until she turned into her driveway twenty minutes later. She'd been able to think of nothing but Clint.

That evening she gathered her courage and phoned his home, certain he would return from his trip that evening, certain he would want one last day at the office before leaving. Tomorrow was Friday. When there was no answer, she felt deflated. Having worked herself up to call him, she found his not being there anticlimactic.

Back in the living room she sat down to read, but her mind wandered. She recalled Clint's demand that she do some thinking about them. He wasn't to know she had done little else.

She pressed her fingers to her lips. She couldn't let him go, she just couldn't! She had to make a last-ditch effort to try and understand his motives. Despite his oblique reference to a lot happening in six months, perhaps time was what they needed—a separation of months, with their marriage then taking place if they both felt the same way.

It was a gamble, uncertain as she was about his feelings for her. She knew, with an ever-growing conviction, that she must heed the dictates of her heart, pride and reason notwithstanding. She loved him too much.

Maybe she had been overcautious, expecting declarations from Clint while being unbending herself. If she made this suggestion to him, surely he would realize how difficult it was for her to take the initiative, to admit she cared for him enough to contemplate marrying him at all. It was contrary to all she had said and done. She was, as it were, putting her pride on the back burner.

Suddenly she could hardly wait for him to come home, couldn't wait to speak to him.

She picked up a paperback to read, more content now after having made a decision in tune with her inner desires. The relief made her feel light-headed. She glanced at her mother, tempted to tell her of her decision, then kept silent. She had better speak to Clint first.

Two hours later Marilyn looked up from her own paperback to ask, "Would you like to watch the 10 o'clock news?"

Debra nodded her agreement.

The news followed the usual pattern of conflict over missiles and toxic wastes. Suddenly Debra tensed.

"The Rasmussen Products' corporate jet is six hours overdue at John Wayne Airport and is presumed to have crashed," the newscaster said. "Search rescue planes will have to wait for daylight before combing the route the plane is thought to have taken."

"No, oh no!" Debra whispered.

Her mother rushed over to put a reassuring arm around her shoulders. "Debra, don't think the worst, dear.

They're bound to find the plane in the morning. Perhaps Clint isn't on that plane."

Hope flickered within Debra. Then she shook her head. "Who else would be using it?" she asked, voice rising. "His father is overseas and used the scheduled airlines." She ran to the phone. "I've got to find out."

"Calm down, Debra!" Marilyn cried, rushing after her. "Why, you're positively shaking!"

Her mother's worried voice hardly penetrated. Fear had Debra in its grip; she could feel hysteria rising within her and fought desperately for control.

Hands trembling, she dialed the airport. The phone rang on and on.

"Oh God, answer— Somebody!"

"Debra, dear," her mother intervened anxiously.

Debra shook her head, warning her mother someone had answered. "Hello! Is Clint Rasmussen on the plane— the Rasmussen corporate jet—that's crashed?"

The infuriatingly calm voice on the other end told her to hold as her call was transferred to the appropriate person who might have that information. Once again Debra repeated her question, tripping over her words in her haste.

"I'm sorry, Miss, we have no verification yet as to whether the plane has crashed," the man said. "I'm not at liberty to disclose the passenger list at the moment, except to next of kin."

Debra groaned. "I—I'm his fiancée, Debra McLeod." God forgive her for that white lie. "Please," she begged with a sob, "please tell me if Clint Rasmussen is on the plane."

"I'd like to help you, Miss McLeod, I really would but, ah, look here's a number you can call. Perhaps you'll learn something there."

Debra felt her heart almost stop. She turned a face full of hope to her mother, who was hovering at her side.

"Dear heaven, he can't be on the plane after all! They've given me Clint's number to call. He must have come home after I phoned. Oh, Mom!" She turned back to the phone. "Thank you, thank you very much!"

Her heart felt as if it would jump from her as she dialed Clint's number. This time the phone only rang once before it was answered by a breathless, anxious, "Hello."

It was a woman's voice. For a moment Debra almost hung up. Clint was home, he had to be. While she had been frantic with worry, he'd been entertaining another woman!

But she had to know for sure if he was all right. "This is Debra McLeod," she said in a rush, pushing aside pride and suspicion. "Is Clint there? I heard on the news that the company plane had possibly crashed and—"

"Debra, this is Laurie. Yes, Clint is on the plane. I waited at the airport for hours, then came here. Clint gave me his key before he left and when...when he returns, he's bound to come here first." Laurie's voice broke.

Debra came close to fainting then, hardly aware she was twisting the telephone cord. "May I...may I come and wait with you?" How she got the words out she didn't know, her brain numb with terror.

"Certainly."

There was no hesitancy in Laurie's voice, no question as to why she should intrude at this time of family crisis. Maybe Clint had told his sister that they had been seeing each other, that a relationship, of sorts, had grown between them. Whatever the reason, Debra was grateful.

When she arrived at Clint's house some time later, it felt natural for Laurie and her to greet each other as if they were old friends.

Laurie looked wan and frightened and very young. In spite of her own anxiety, Debra immediately felt she had to try and reassure Laurie that Clint was safe.

"They only think the plane may have crashed," she told the younger girl. "It isn't a fact." Unfortunately her quivering tone did little to impart the reassurance she'd intended.

"I keep telling myself that, too, but I can't help worrying!" Laurie exclaimed. She looked like she was about to cry.

Impulsively Debra hugged her. "We've got to hope for the best. That's all we can do." Her own voice broke, and she struggled to keep the tears at bay as she and Laurie sat on the sofa and prepared to wait all night if need be.

As Debra surreptitiously wiped a tear from her face, Laurie asked softly, "Are you in love with my brother, Debra?"

Her head bowed, Debra didn't hesitate in her reply. "Yes, yes I am." Right now she'd admit the truth to anyone, no matter what happened later, as long as Clint came home, safe and well. She wanted nothing more.

"I should have guessed," Laurie mused. "And I was dumb enough to accuse you of still loving Brian."

Debra couldn't even think of Brian at this time. "If anything happens to Clint, I don't know what I'll do," she whispered. "Dear Lord, it just can't happen!"

"My brother's a resourceful man. He'll be okay, I'm sure of it."

Debra detected the bravado in Laurie's voice. She herself felt a hard knot of fear gripping her stomach, but for Laurie's sake, she had to try to remain calm. She gave one last wipe of her eyes, then lifted her head.

"I'm a firm believer in positive thinking, too," she said, striving for a note of firmness. *But, oh, it's never been so sorely tested before,* she added silently.

Laurie nodded. "It helps, doesn't it?"

Debra managed a nod in return and tried to ignore the pressure of tears behind her eyes.

"Um, Debra...about Brian and me. I—I didn't mean to tell Clint, but I was alone and crying one evening when he came over to see us, and I blurted out the whole miserable mess."

Relief washed over Debra. "I'm glad. I know he'll want to help you."

"I realize that." Laurie's pretty face was somber. "Would you believe it, Brian's already seeing another woman?"

"How could he!"

"Don't be distressed on my account. I acted stupidly and I'm paying for it." Laurie looked older in that moment, and Debra's heart ached for her. "I also have good reason to believe he married me because of Dad's money."

"Oh, Laurie." Debra didn't know what else to say. She'd had her own suspicions about Brian's motives for marrying Laurie from the minute he'd said that he didn't love Laurie. Laurie's suspicion could be the only possible reason. It was despicable, but Debra could believe it of Brian.

Laurie laced her fingers together and gave her a tiny, self-conscious smile. "Clint didn't come right out and say 'I told you so' but it was what he was thinking." She shifted uncomfortably on the sofa. "I'm back home again. Clint didn't even try to advise me to work things out with Brian, which surprised me. It shows that his opinion of Brian must be pretty low."

"I see."

Debra's reactions were mixed. Despite the prevalence of divorce, she'd always thought of marriage as lasting a lifetime. Certainly she wanted that for herself, but didn't every woman? In the circumstances, Laurie's easy dismissal of her marriage should have shocked her. But it didn't. If it had been any man other than Brian involved, she would have encouraged Laurie to try to salvage her marriage, to work at saving it. But knowing Brian, she couldn't in good conscience do that, and it saddened her.

Was Clint's quick acceptance of the breakup of Laurie's marriage motivated by the same reasoning? Or did he not have to do any wrestling with his own beliefs? Did he just not place the same importance on the sanctity of marriage as she did?

"Heavens, I'm tired," Laurie said with a yawn, "but I don't want to lie down in case the phone rings."

"Look, why don't you lie down on Clint's bed while I stay here? I'll hear the phone."

Laurie appeared uncertain for a moment, but Debra managed to persuade her to do as she suggested. The instant Laurie disappeared into the bedroom, Debra slipped off her shoes and propped herself up with some cushions, half reclining on the sofa, her mind alert, her ears straining.

The two table lamps shed a soft glow over the spacious room that now seemed so terribly empty without Clint there to tease her, to hold her. She could feel tears welling, and she blinked, but silent tears slid down her face anyway.

Somehow, she had to get through this night. Midnight came and went, and so did one o'clock and two. The hours ticked by, long, slow and torturous. Finally she curled deeper into the mounds of cushions. Although she was physically comfortable, her mind made relaxation impossible. Over and over she told herself Clint was safe. He had to be!

What if he was lying somewhere, injured, needing medical attention? Tears again welled, and this time they slid down her face in such profusion that her cheeks were sopping. Silently she prayed for Clint's safe return, more earnestly than she had ever prayed for anyone in her life, her lips mouthing the words, her muffled sobs disrupting the quiet of the room.

Though she was certain she couldn't, she must have dozed off. A slight clicking sound wakened her. She struggled upright and pressed a hand to her chest. Was that the front door she had heard?

Shoeless, she stumbled to the hall and rounded the corner at full tilt, her body colliding with that of a tall, powerfully built man. She gasped and flung her arms around his neck. And for one euphoric, unguarded moment, Clint held her close.

"Clint, oh Clint!" she cried, and her eyes searched his face anxiously in the dim light. Never before had she seen him so drained. There was a bandage on his head, and an ugly stain of blood that made her shiver with fright. "You're hurt," she whispered, clutching at his shoulders.

He removed her hands and set her away from him. "What are you doing here?" he asked.

She froze. "I—I heard about the plane crash." She wet her lips. "Laurie said I could stay," she added, suddenly defensive. Her hand went out to touch him, but she stopped herself in time. "Are you all right?"

"Never better." He walked away from her, and she hurried after him as he headed straight for the liquor cabinet in the living room.

She cringed inwardly at his sarcasm and his obvious displeasure at her presence. Still, the heartfelt relief that he

was here, standing before her, alive and apparently not
seriously injured, made her close her eyes a second and
give thanks. When she opened her eyes, she noticed he had
discarded his tie and that his suit was rumpled. She'd never
seen him disheveled before, but oh, he looked good to her.

Clint filled his glass and stared back at her, a derisive
curl to his lips. "I'll live," he said in a more reasonable
tone. "There's no need for this concern, if that's what's
brought you here."

"Clint I—"

"Clint, you've alive!" Laurie ran from the bedroom.
"What happened?"

"Hello, little one." Clint's grim expression disappeared
as he bestowed an affectionate smile on his sister and
kissed her cheek.

It tore at Debra's insides to witness Clint's loving greeting with his sister in such sharp contrast to his coldness
toward her. She immediately felt ashamed of the unbid-
den thought. Still, except for the few moments when he
had first stepped into the hall, he had treated her as if she
had no business here, as if she were an uninvited and ex-
tremely unwanted guest.

She felt crushed, yet made no move to leave. Instead she
joined Clint and Laurie as they sat down.

"Our plane had engine trouble," Clint directed his ex-
planation toward Laurie. "We lost radio contact as well,
but Bob, my pilot, did a terrific job bringing us down in a
field. We were lucky in that we still had some daylight.
After that we walked for a couple of hours until we came
to a farm house and hired the owner to drive us here."

"But why didn't you phone the airport, or Laurie,
or... or me?" Debra exclaimed.

Clint's only acknowledgement of her was a sardonic
lifting of one eyebrow. Then his gaze again turned to his

sister. "The phone lines were down." He rubbed the stubble on his chin. "They'd had some high winds in the area. Anyway, Bob and I didn't want to waste time. We were anxious to get home, but I was bleeding, and we had to stop at a hospital emergency room. I was feeling a bit rough, but I'm sure he phoned the airport then. Anyway, after I was patched up, we came on here, dropping Bob off at his place first."

"Just so long as you're okay." Laurie sent an anxious glance at his bandage.

Debra got to her feet. "I must be going." She avoided looking at Clint lest he see in her eyes the love she felt. To guess by his demeanor, their personal relationship no longer existed. As for marriage, such thoughts seemed irrelevant now. It was hard to imagine the same man had told her to think about their future, let alone had proposed.

"Yes, I must be going, too," Laurie said briskly, then smiled over at Debra. "Let's hope next time we meet, it won't be another crisis."

Debra nodded; she couldn't smile no matter how hard she tried. She was too close to tears. She lifted her shoulder bag; and although Laurie seemed in a hurry to leave, Debra found her own feet slow to follow the dictates of her brain. Just as she had reached the open doorway, Clint detained her.

His hand on her arm would not have stopped her if she had wanted to leave, his touch was so light. Perhaps her hesitation provided him with a measure of encouragement, for without a word he closed the front door after Laurie left.

"Why did you come tonight, Debra? What was it, friendly concern?"

"You know it was more than that," she answered in a low, tight voice. "I don't normally sit up all night, or a good part of it, worrying over a casual friend."

He touched her cheek. "Is that what you did, honey?"

She didn't answer, her response to his light touch making her hands shake. By tacit agreement she and Clint returned to the living room, where she stepped away from him, much as she wanted to have him hold her and kiss her. So far he hadn't so much as given her a peck on the cheek. Even his sister had rated that much.

"Suppose you tell me why you did come, then," he drawled.

He wasn't going to make it easy for her. She'd refused him; now he wanted her recapitulation. Difficult as it made things for her, she couldn't blame him.

She walked to the window. There was a streak of light in the sky; daybreak was not far off. She wished with all her heart Clint would give some indication he still wanted to marry her, but he didn't. He had told her he would ask her once, and only once. It was up to her.

She felt chilled suddenly, and doubled her cardigan across her chest. She couldn't look at him but was aware of him, inches away, at her back.

"I've thought about us as you asked me to," she began, trying desperately to sound matter-of-fact. "If you still want me to, I'll marry you, but not right away. We could marry when you return in six months," she added quickly, in a hurry to have her say while she still had the nerve. "That will give us, both of us, time to be sure."

He swore softly behind her, and his hand was ungentle as he swung her to face him. "That damn pride of yours won't let you make a full-fledged commitment, will it, Debra? You have to have the door open a crack so you can slip through."

She looked up into his unyielding face. "That's not true!" The despair she felt was obvious in her voice.

"Isn't it? Well, no matter, your plan doesn't suit me. You either want to marry me, or you don't. You marry me now, today, or we don't marry at all."

Chapter Eleven

The shock of his ultimatum made her heart palpitate, and she bit down hard on her full lower lip. Temper flashed through her; the urge to tell him, quite explicitly, where he could go with his brusque proposal, trembled on her lips. But one look at his face and she knew if she told him to go to hell, he might very well take her with him.

How she hated his arrogant confidence! The ruthless inflexibility of his voice made it clear he had dealt his last card. She could fight against the intangible bonds that bound her to him all she wanted, but they held her prisoner. She couldn't let him walk out of her life. Perhaps he was banking on that, but there was no telling from his expression.

He had said she would have to make her decision with her head. Well, she certainly couldn't accuse him of using the physical chemistry that vibrated between them as an inducement. In some ways, she wished he would. It would make her acceptance easier if she could make excuses for herself by blaming her surrender on desire, even though she knew full well it was much more than that. Despite his proposal, there was nothing of the lover in his attitude; yet the love she bore him conquered that momentary impulse to denounce him.

He looked a bit gray about the lips, and her conscience reminded her that she was keeping him standing, arguing with her, after the ordeal he had been through.

"You should be in bed," she murmured. She flinched at Clint's sudden shrewd appraisal. Hot color stained her cheeks.

"You haven't answered me, Debra." His eyes were watchful. "Quit stalling."

She inhaled deeply, then threw back her head, tousled auburn waves shining in the glow from the lamps. "Yes, I'll marry you, Clint," she replied with only a hint of a tremor in her voice.

She could actually feel the deep sigh shudder through him, the harsh lines of fatigue about his mouth seeming to vanish. For one blissful moment he drew her close, and she felt his lips on her temple.

"You won't regret it, sweetheart. I promise you."

She waited for words of love, but none came, and her fragile emotions after the traumatic night caused moisture to gather at the back of her eyes. Her love was entrenched within her, for now and forever; but what Clint felt remained obscure, except for desire, of course.

She'd make him love her, she vowed silently. He just had to!

Without a word, Clint released her and went immediately to the phone. Any thoughts of going to bed appeared shelved as he arranged for a charter plane to take them to Las Vegas. Her head was spinning at the speed with which he was putting his plans into effect. A bubble

of hysteria surged in her throat. Trust Clint not even to
wait for a scheduled flight. He seemed to have shed his
weariness. When he indicated he wanted to shower and
change before leaving, she suggested she drive home and
do the same. To her astonishment, he immediately objected.

"Oh no you don't. I'll take you home. I don't want you
out of my sight any more than absolutely necessary."

"I won't walk out on you." Nerves made her snap.
"You needn't be afraid of that."

"I'm not afraid, Debra," he came back shortly, "but
I'm not taking any chances."

She could have left while he was in the shower, but
didn't. It was a scant ten minutes before he rejoined her in
the living room. He had changed into the impeccably tailored gray suit he had worn at the wedding when they first
met. He'd replaced the bandage on his head with a huge
plaster, but even so he looked fabulous, and her stomach
turned over at the thought they would soon be husband
and wife.

Next thing she knew he had whisked her home. Together they told her mother of their plans. She was overjoyed.

"You'll come with us, Marilyn?" Clint smiled and
pulled Debra against his side. "I'm sure you want to attend your daughter's wedding."

Love rose inside Debra, almost suffocating her. She
knew Clint's first instincts had been to spirit her away, get
married, and tell everyone else afterward. Certainly he
hadn't phoned Laurie. But her mother was special, and if
he hadn't invited her, she would have.

"Oh, dear!" Marilyn exclaimed, obviously distressed.
"I'm at the shop on my own today. Couldn't you post-

oone the wedding?'' She asked the question of Clint, her
face clouding as he shook his head.

''We're scheduled to fly to London on Monday, Mari-
yn.''

He sounded truly regretful, while Debra was struck
dumb, assimilating that he apparently expected her to go
with him, but hadn't even bothered to mention his plans
to her. Everything was happening so fast that she felt her
life was slipping rapidly out of control. For a second she
thought of the new job she was supposed to start on Monday, then forgot it when Clint looked down at her, his lazy
smile driving all else from her mind but him.

''You'd better get packed, love,'' he murmured, and
gave her a slight push toward the stairs.

Whatever he said while she was changing placated her
mother somewhat, for when they were leaving, Marilyn
hugged and kissed them both goodbye, smiling through the
few glad tears one could expect from the mother of the
bride.

Once in the car, Debra smoothed down the cream chif-
fon of her dress, the only dress she had that was anything
bridelike. Her hands trembled. ''I never thought I'd get
married in Vegas. I always pictured a church wedding, too.
It seems more binding.''

But then, Clint didn't care whether it was binding or not.
She felt an utter fool for expressing her thoughts. She
looked out the side window and hoped he couldn't see her
lips quivering, a dead giveaway of her emotional upheaval.

''There's no time for frills, Debra.'' His voice gave
nothing away. ''Later we can have another ceremony, a
reception, whatever you want. Make no mistake, though,
this service will be binding. You'll be my wife.''

Then why can't you say you love me? she cried silently.

No such declaration was forthcoming, and the silence between them became stifling. She was glad when they arrived at Orange County's John Wayne Airport, glad of the hustle and bustle of people hurrying to early-morning flights.

It was turning into a gorgeous day, the sun bright overhead, and some of her misgivings abated. Not all, by any means, but it was impossible to look on the black side, to worry about future problems when Mother Nature was putting forth her best effort.

Clint certainly did everything with panache, she mused, as he helped her buckle her seat belt. The Learjet's interior was luxurious, and Clint assured her they'd have breakfast once they were airborne. When she murmured she didn't feel hungry, he gave her a worried frown.

They arrived at Las Vegas long before she was ready, mentally or emotionally. A chauffeur-driven limousine was waiting for them, and Clint sat in the back with her. He didn't try to make small talk, just held her hand in his. Although she still questioned his true feeling for her, she found that contact between them comforting.

There was no more time for fence-sitting, no more time for backing out. She was shaking so much when Clint helped her from the limousine that he made an impatient sound in his throat.

"You're going to be married," he said in an undertone, "not executed."

"I can't help it," she whispered right back as they walked up the path to the tiny chapel.

He shook his head, the glint of annoyance turning to amusement. "You'll feel better afterward, honey, I promise."

She threw him a look and refused to answer, making him chuckle as he ushered her indoors. After that, every hing happened so quickly she hadn't time to think. She vas presented with an exquisite bouquet of yellow roses, nd ten minutes later they were exchanging vows.

Automatically, as if she had rehearsed her part, she ifted her face for his kiss at the appropriate moment. Her ips felt cold and stiff beneath the warmth of his. Clint rowned slightly into her pale face, then turned her about.

"Smile for the camera, Debra."

Startled, she became aware for the first time of a pho- ographer lingering nearby. She tried to do as Clint said, out her lips felt stretched over her teeth; there was no pontaneity. She was scared, pure and simple. If Clint had oved her, this moment would have been ecstatic. Instead he felt a misery that the elation of being Clint's wife vould not erase.

"We'll go right to our hotel," he said as they stepped outside.

"Haven't you got the decency to wait?" she snapped, hen went white.

He stopped dead, and his fingers dug into her arm a econd before he let his hand fall to his side. "Let's get one hing straight. I am not dragging you to a hotel to have my wicked way with you," he mocked. "No matter what you hink, I am not a sex-starved maniac."

"I never said you were," she retorted, flushing. She sent a warning glance at the limousine where the chauffeur waited, out of hearing, she hoped.

With a grimace, Clint followed the direction of her glance. "You're the one who started this, Debra, so don't get uptight when I finish it." His arm slipped around her waist, even though his irritation was obvious. "You're tired, you've had a worrisome night and a hectic morn- ng. I merely thought you'd like a nap."

With or without him for company? One look at his fac[e]
and she decided not to ask the question. His concer[n]
seemed genuine, and suddenly she felt small. "I'm sorry[,]
Clint. I guess I'm suffering from bridal nerves."

"Perhaps."

The chauffeur stood smartly at attention as they got i[n]
the backseat, and once again Clint took her hand in hi[s.]
Strangely enough, that brief heated exchange had r[e-]
leased some of her pent-up tension, and Debra relaxe[d]
slightly as the limousine traveled away from the gamblin[g]
strip with its neon signs and heavy traffic. Nerves over[-]
came her again, though, when the limousine turned int[o]
the long circular driveway of a small hotel on the out[-]
skirts of the city. She was too worked up again to even n[o-]
tice the name, but the discreet good taste of th[e]
establishment was immediately evident.

After a minimum of formalities at the reservation desk[,]
she and Clint were escorted to their suite. The first thin[g]
that hit her gaze was a huge round bed, covered in a sati[n]
spread of delicate ecru with insets of lace in the generou[s]
flounce. The bed dominated the room. She was only hal[f]
aware of a velvet chaise longue and sundry other pieces o[f]
white and gold furniture in the French style. Numerou[s]
plants stood out lushly green amongst such pastels. Th[e]
overall effect was charmingly romantic.

While Clint tipped the porter, she tried to calm down b[y]
going out on the balcony. The garden was filled with dat[e]
palms interspersed with fountains and brilliant purple an[d]
red bougainvillea. The scene was one of complete tran[-]
quility and loveliness.

She felt a hand on her shoulder, and in the next instan[t]
Clint had turned her around and kissed her lightly on th[e]
mouth. It was a careful, controlled kiss, and she coul[d]
sense he was trying not to unnerve her further. H[e]

houghtfulness made the love rush through her. She smiled
p at him, a wide, generous smile. His hands on her
houlders tensed, and he pulled her closer.

A tap on the door stopped the slow descent of his head.
With a resigned grin at her, he went to answer it, return-
ng with a huge gold-and-white-trimmed package, which
.e handed to her.

"My goodness, what's this?" she exclaimed.

"Open it and you'll find out," he returned indulgently.

She read what turned out to be his gift card, and ea-
erly removed layers and layers of white tissue before dis-
overing a white peignoir set of shimmering satin and
ppliquéd lace.

"Oh, Clint, how utterly beautiful," she breathed, lift-
ng a bright, if pink, face to his. "How—"

He circled her nape with one hand. "I made a few phone
alls from your house while you were changing. Some-
imes it helps to have a few connections," he said. "Every
•ride, mine especially, has a right to something pretty to
vear on her wedding night."

"You didn't give me time to plan anything," she pro-
ested with a small pout.

"You've had all the time you're going to get, Mrs. Ras-
nussen."

Her new name gave her a distinct thrill, although she
•urposely overlooked the intent of Clint's words. With the
eductive rubbing of his thumb along the side of her neck,
nothing else seemed to matter. Instinctively she rested her
•alms on his chest and tilted back her head, but when her
yes met the burning need in his she faltered, overcome by
. mixture of fear and expectation.

"Don't lose your nerve, honey." Clint's hand slid down
er back to her waist and drew her closer. "There's no
need to hold back anymore."

She stepped right away from him. "I, ah, think I'll have that nap you suggested."

"Go right ahead. I might have one myself." He looked amused by her immediately suspicious look. "I had a rough night myself last night, if you remember."

"As if I'll ever forget!"

She felt contrite for not taking this into account. All she could think about was that he might not wait until the night to make love to her; and the more she thought about it, the more panicky she became. He'd once said he wanted to be the first man to teach her about love, and so he would be; but would she, in her inexperience, be able to satisfy him? Would he regret marrying her?

Her legs felt as though they might give way beneath her as she hurried to her suitcase on the luggage rack. She'd hang up her dress and lie down in her robe. She certainly wouldn't put on that exquisite nightgown. Not now, not in the middle of the day with the sun blazing through the windows.

Yet she hesitated as she was about to pass the box containing Clint's gift. She'd be uncomfortable lying down half-clothed, she told herself, and whipped the silken gown and gossamer negligee over her arm and hastened into the bathroom before she could change her mind or analyze her actions.

She showered, conscious of the warm water running over her body stimulating her sensual responses. She delighted in the rose scent of the soap and bath powder provided, and the softness of the thick fluffy towel.

It was all wrong, though, she told herself as she felt the exquisite gown slip over her bareness; and that thought took some of the sparkle from her eyes, a sparkle put there by Clint's thoughtfulness, of his realizing she would want something pretty for her wedding night. She had every le

ll right to sleep in Clint's bed, but what about moral
ghts? She couldn't pretend he loved her. She was the ob-
ct of his desire, nothing more. She groaned and covered
er face with her hands. Why did she have to love him so
uch? In spite of everything, she longed for him with an
che that was excruciating, her mind and emotions
onstantly at war.

Her hands shook as she slipped on the negligee, and she
eeded several deep breaths before she had the courage to
pen the door and reenter the bedroom. The room was
arker than when she had left it. Sunlight filtered across
ne floor beneath the now-closed drapes. Her teeth wor-
ed her lower lip. Clint was lying on the bed, the spread
d light blanket neatly turned over at the foot.

Her heart thumped in her chest as she neared him. She
raced herself to appear poised should he make some
easing remark or try to coax her down beside him. He did
either, and for a very good reason. He was sound asleep!

Surprise and relief almost made her giggle aloud. She
as getting a reprieve, so why did she feel let down? He
adn't slept in over thirty-six hours; it was natural he
ould doze off the instant he lay down. She bent over
m, thinking she had never seen Clint like this, his face in
pose, younger, even vulnerable with that plaster on his
rehead. Did his head hurt? she wondered anxiously.

He'd removed his tie, jacket and shoes, but otherwise
as clothed. It seemed she had no reason to feel threat-
ed, not yet anyway.

She tiptoed around to the other side of the bed. After
refully spreading her negligee over the chaise longue, she
y down gingerly beside him so as not to waken him, not
ecause of her apprehension of what might follow if she
id, but because he needed the rest.

Perhaps it wasn't surprising that with all that had tra
spired, she fell asleep quickly, a deep dreamless sleep fro
which she didn't awaken until hours later.

"Hello there, sleepyhead," a deep baritone drawled b
side her, and she opened her eyes to find Clint leaning
his elbow and staring down at her.

"H-hello." How long had he been staring down at h
for goodness' sake. If Clint could look vulnerable while l
slept, what secrets of hers had he guessed at while watc
ing her? She blinked, refocusing her eyes to the dim ligl
Then came the second shock. His upper torso gleamed; l
was naked except for a minuscule towel around his wai
Suddenly she felt she would suffocate, and her eyes dart
away from his. The light shining beneath the drapes w
artificial now, lamps from the garden, probably. "It mu
be late." Her voice was hoarse.

"Dinnertime," he agreed, and nuzzled his face into h
neck, feathering tiny kisses against her skin, his hand
her waist holding her firm when she tried to inch away.

"We . . . we'd better go and eat."

He nibbled her earlobe. "There's no rush. There's
rush about anything."

She pushed against his shoulder, then withdrew her ha
as if scalded by the warmth of his skin. Her control slipp
even more as he pressed his devastating, light kisses again
her throat.

Panic, stifling in its intensity, made her tremble when l
hands caressed the silken length of her and followed h
curves and indentations with a knowing expertise that l
her gasping. But despite the sweet languor taking posse
sion of her limbs, doubts still tortured her, and she
tered a soft protest.

Clint's hands stilled, and he lifted his head. "Wha
wrong, sweetheart?"

She swallowed, but no words came. Instead she buried her head in his bare shoulder.

"Not talking to me, Debra?" A smile in his voice, he chuckled softly when she shook her head. He moved suddenly, reaching behind her to turn on the bedside lamp, then gently tipped up her chin with his forefinger.

"You don't still have doubts, do you?" he asked incredulously when he saw her face.

She made herself meet his eyes. "I know this marriage is a travesty, a short-term, legal affair. Nothing more." Her voice was barely above a whisper and shook with emotion. "You wanted to go to bed with me, and this was the only way to get what you wanted."

"My God, woman, you can't believe that!"

Clint looked shaken, not angry as she had expected him to be when she confronted him with her knowledge. But, oh, how she wished he hadn't turned on the lamp when she felt a teardrop she couldn't withhold slip down her face. Ever so tenderly Clint wiped it away with his thumb.

"You little idiot," he murmured when she remained silent. "I assure you it took more than physical desire to get this wily bachelor married." He smiled into her troubled green eyes in a way that made her heart turn over. "I love you, Mrs. Rasmussen, body and soul, until death do us part."

She gulped, overcome. "All this time, you—you never once said you loved me," she whispered accusingly.

"Every time I came close to declaring myself, you took off on a tangent about my supposed misdeeds," he reminded her dryly. "And whenever I tried to get a commitment from you, you balked. I was never sure how you really felt until you actually went through with our marriage."

She bent her head, swallowing once again over the painful dryness of her throat. "And . . . and how do you think I feel?"

"You tell me, Debra."

There was sternness in his voice. She knew he wanted her to cross over the gulf of misunderstandings and pride that had kept them apart. But she had to ask one more question that was nagging at her subconscious.

She looked up, anxious to gauge his reaction to what she was about to say. "What . . . what if I had refused to agree to your ultimatum?" she asked, still chafing at his final take-it-or-leave-it proposal. "Would you really have left and never bothered with me again?"

He sighed, his smile rueful. "I'd probably have left in disgust, but I would have come back. I had to take the gamble that if you loved me, you'd marry me, that you wouldn't ruin both our lives over stupid pride."

He fell silent, waiting.

Debra knew then what she must do. She wrapped one arm around his neck and drew his head down until his lips were no more than an inch from her own. "I love you, Clint Rasmussen," she vowed solemnly, "for now and forever."

"Oh, sweetheart, I've waited so long to hear you say that."

With a deft move, he switched off the lamp; then he gathered her close, his lips on hers drawing such a response from her that she felt faint with the wonder of it. When his hand slipped aside her flimsy shoulder strap, she once again trembled, but this time with anticipation. A strangled gasp came from her when he cupped her breast and stroked the nipple. Breathing his name into his mouth, she felt the new urgency in his kisses, the possessiveness of his hands on her body. She felt drugged by kisses and caresses that both tantalized and demanded. For all his saying that there was no rush, he soon disposed of her dainty gown and tossed it carelessly aside.

His hard, muscular shoulders beneath her palms filled her with indescribable craving; the clean male scent of him heightened emotions already spiraling. It was feminine instinct, not knowledge, that made her body arch to meet the seeking of his lips on her breasts, his touch arousing a sweet torment within her and a soft cry of pleasure.

Her love cry aroused a deep sound of male satisfaction from Clint as his hands cupped and stroked the curve of her hips, even while they urged her forward. Her brain warned her she should tell him she'd never known a man, not this way, but the blood roaring in her ears drowned out caution. All she was aware of was the fiery response his lips and hands were inciting within her, of the driving need that made her convulsively dig her nails into his shoulders, her desire to be closer, despite her trepidation, matching his. Her slim arms had a will of their own and tightened around his neck, inviting his possession.

The pain, when it came, made her eyes glaze with shock, but her scream was cut off by the hot demand of Clint's mouth.

"God, why didn't you tell me?" he asked moments later when he lifted his head. Without waiting for an answer, he claimed her lips again, this time gently, but insistently, as insistent as the hands that held her captive beneath him, the rhythm of his body slower now, evoking a response from the very depth of her soul. Pain merged with ecstasy, and hands that had tried to push him away, clung.

Afterward, her body limp and her mind dazed, she allowed him to enfold her within his arms, her head on his broad shoulder, her hand on his dampened chest. When she shivered, he drew the light blanket over them and pressed his lips to her temple.

"So I was the first," he murmured against her skin.

She was too shaken by the explosion of feeling he had aroused within her to find a pert reply. What's more, she knew now that her fears that she might disappoint him were unfounded.

She stroked his chest, glorying in her right and privilege to do so, and loving the feel of him. "I—I guess it sounds corny in these times to say this, but I always promised myself I'd wait for the right man." She wanted to add that when he had possessed her body, he had possessed all of her; but a sudden shyness overcame her, and she fell silent.

"Oh, my beautiful, beautiful wife." His arms tightened around her. "I'm glad, so glad, that you waited for me."

There was a humble note in his voice; and Debra, never having heard quite that tone in his voice before, raised her head to look up at him.

What she saw in his eyes made her catch her breath. There was love, yes, but there was awe as well. He appeared in the grip of an emotion so overpowering that his normal self-assurance seemed to have deserted him.

"I'll make you happy, sweetheart," he said. "I—I promise you. Anything...anything you want, it's yours."

She smiled softly at his fervency and brushed her lips across his.

"I have all I want, my darling, right here. Oh, except for maybe a baby or two."

"I'll see what I can do about that," he promised.

And as their lips met, she knew deep in her heart that her husband would keep his promise.

*   *   *   *   *